ABOUT THIS BOOK

Seventeen-year-old Serena Alverson is drawn to water. She spends much of her time by the falls, sketching the beauty of life's sustenance. An introverted "late bloomer," she has no interest in a social life aside from her two best friends, Logan and Nikki. She's never had a serious boyfriend and has rarely left the safety of Havenwood Falls.

Serena has big dreams for her future, things she wants for herself after high school—to travel and study the great artists of the world while developing her own craft. To break free from the sleepy little town she outgrew by age eight. But her carefully laid plans fall asunder when she receives a gift from her aunt, a mysterious necklace with the power to sear her skin. With each burn, she questions her sanity. It doesn't help that an ominous figure starts shadowing her steps.

When Mother Nature finally comes knocking, she hands Serena not only her womanhood, but also a wicked lifetime curse with the potential to destroy everything and everyone she loves. For water also has a dark side. Water is birth, water is life . . . water is death.

THE FALL

A HAVENWOOD FALLS HIGH NOVELLA

KRISTEN YARD

HAVENWOOD FALLS HIGH BOOKS

Written in the Stars by Kallie Ross
Reawakened by Morgan Wylie
The Fall by Kristen Yard
Somewhere Within by Amy Hale
Awaken the Soul by Michele G. Miller

More books releasing on a monthly basis

Stay up to date at www.HavenwoodFalls.com

Published by

Ang'dora Productions, LLC

5621 Strand Blvd, Ste 210

Naples, FL 34110

Havenwood Falls and Ang'dora Productions and their associated logos are trademarks and/or registered trademarks of Ang'dora Productions, LLC.

Cover design by Regina Wamba at MaeIDesign.com

Ebook ISBN: 978-1-939859-43-3

Print ISBN: 978-1-939859-44-0

For Alexa
My love for you is water.
Undying, life-giving,
in this world and beyond—always.

If you are falling…dive.

~ Joseph Campbell

CHAPTER 1

*L*ight glimmers through the ceiling of a cavern. Moonlight morphs the water into a sea of diamonds, bobbing gently against rock walls. Water roars in the distance. I sit up, assessing the situation.

Where am I?

How did I wind up in a cave, when I swear I just laid my head down for a quick couch nap? Glancing down at my bare feet, I note the dirt on them. *Where are my shoes?*

I steady myself and then rise to my feet, looking for an exit, but there isn't one. My heart ricochets off my rib cage as I run my hands along the wall, edging my toes over the tiny strip of stone separating me from the water.

"Help!" I call, sifting through memories of the day, trying to piece together what could have led to this.

School, then a Coffee Haven stop with my best friend, Nikki Morris, and her new boyfriend, Max Cooper, then home, and couch.

So how am I here? And what is this place?

My mind flashes to the lagoon behind the tiny distributary waterfall that runs from Havenwood Falls into my own backyard, but the lagoon looks nothing like this. There is definitely an exit to that cavern.

My hands go clammy. Max was the one who grabbed our coffees from the barista and brought them to the table. Logan Andrews, my and Nikki's other best friend, is convinced that Max brought not only designer clothes, but also designer drugs with him when he moved here from New York City.

He drugged us. That's it. Oh my God. Nikki.

Whatever fear I have for my own well-being takes a back seat to the throat-tightening terror of picturing my bestie tied up in a trunk —or worse.

"NIKKI!" My voice breaks into a sob. Then I clamp my hands over my mouth, realizing that Max might still be in the vicinity. *What if I got away and am now luring him back to finish me off? No. I have to find a way out and call for help.*

Losing my footing, I slide down onto my knees, my arms flailing out to catch me before I fall into the lagoon.

I fight to catch my breath and then notice a sound that picks up over the surrounding cacophony of rushing water.

Whispers. Layers of them, building upon one another.

I freeze, trying to focus in, past the rushing falls, so that I can understand what they are saying. All the while, my mind begs me to run, but I cannot move.

The whispers finally come together into one voice.

"Serenaaaaaa."

It comes directly from the water in front of me. With a gulp, I take a breath and then lean forward, until I am directly over the brackish pool.

The inky clouds clear. An emerald light shines from below the surface, revealing a woman in the depths. Her blond hair cascades around her in waves, concealing her face.

I lean in closer, and the current finally moves enough of her flaxen strands that I can make out her features. A porcelain face with a pointy chin, long eyelashes, a slightly turned-up nose, and full, pink lips. The birthmark on her left cheek sends my heart stuttering, but when her eyes snap open, revealing piercing blue irises, I scream.

Because the girl in the water is me.

Her eyes glow. She shoots up, water droplets glittering around her.

She smirks and then pulls me in, as I scream and kick, trying to break free.

"Serena? Serena!" Aunt Odette yells, as I attempt punching my way to freedom. "Hey! Million Dollar Baby! It's just me, your adorable aunt, trying to wake you up to give you cake and presents. Can you please refrain from killing me?"

I blink a couple of times. The warm glow of the fireplace and the log walls of my family's cabin releases the knot in my stomach.

"You feeling okay, honey?" Aunt Odette's face eclipses my view of the room. Her sky-blue eyes narrow in concern, and she places a hand on my forehead.

"Yeah . . . just a wicked nightmare."

"You want to talk about it?" she asks, rubbing my shoulder.

I shudder. "No, I'm good."

Slowly, I sit up and stretch, shaking the dream off. "So, what's this you said about cake? And did you make it yourself?" I ask, eyeing her, because I love my aunt, but she cannot cook to save her life.

She grins. "Yes, I did. But no worries. I've been practicing! Oh, Serena." She sighs in disapproval.

"What?" I yawn.

"Your feet are filthy. Next time, can you please clean them off before you put them on the furniture?"

The knot returns to my stomach, and I lean over to examine them. My eyes frantically search through the pile of shoes by the door, and I try to remember what I had worn to school. Sandals would explain dirt, but it's too cool for sandals. *It was a dream. How would this even be possible?*

"Okay, okay, I'm sorry for channeling Grandma. That even weirded *me* out," she says, misunderstanding my reaction.

I let out a nervous laugh, and she pulls me to my feet, smoothing my hair.

"And about that cake, oh, ye of little faith. You never know, it could actually be the best of your life." She winks and leads me into the chilly October night.

We walk through our yard, nestled beside Mount Alexa and surrounded by the woods on all sides. Our roaring mini waterfall is a curtain to the lagoon I explored as a little girl, sitting behind our cabin. The thought of it brings me back to the cavern in my nightmare, speeding up my heart, as my mind continues to try making sense of what just happened.

The memory of glowing eyes in the water quickens my pace toward our family's business, the Fallview Grill & Tavern, which is on our property, but higher up the mountain.

"Why are we going here instead of just eating in the house?" I ask.

"Man, are you writing a novel or something? Why all the questions? Maybe I just didn't want to burn the house down. You know, since you think I suck at all things culinary."

"But your heart is in the right place," I offer.

She snorts and then gestures toward the entrance of our restaurant. "Hey, can you open the door? I messed my back up earlier."

"How?" I ask in concern, holding the door open for her to pass.

"SURPRISE!" a group of people shout. I fall back against the door, laughing as my aunt winks.

"Gotcha!" she singsongs, leading me over to the small gathering of our family and friends.

The rustic lodge vibe of the tavern is at odds with the very feminine lavender and silver streamers, balloons, and number-18 decorations strewn about.

Nikki and Logan come up to me first. In the time since we left school this afternoon, Nikki's long wavy brown hair has been hacked into a shoulder-length bob. I gasp as I take it in, flashing Logan a confused look. He barely nods in what I take as quiet agreement that he's as shocked as I am by Nikki's new do.

"Oh!"

"Ya like?" she asks.

I gape at Nikki, because her hair has been one of her most prized physical traits as far back as I can remember.

Her face falls. "You don't like. Clearly."

"*I* don't like," my little sister Laurel pipes up.

Nikki narrows her eyes. "Nobody asked you, Felicia."

"Laurel!" Lena, my other little sister and Laurel's twin, scolds her, as I glare at Laurel. She shrugs. Her white-blond hair shines under the lights as she plops down on the couch and starts texting someone. My phone beeps. I pull it out of my pocket and then turn toward Laurel after reading the text.

"You couldn't just say 'happy birthday' instead of texting it?"

She shrugs again, and Lena comes up and gives me a quick hug.

"Happy birthday, sis."

"Thanks, Bug,"

When I glance up, my best friend still looks aggravated.

"Nikki, I think your hair is adorable. You just caught everyone by surprise," I protest, wrapping my arms around her.

"Happy birthday, babe," she says, kissing my cheek.

Honestly, Nikki's new look does frame her pixie-like features, high cheekbones, and doe eyes to perfection. It's just that she has been undergoing some pretty weird and major personality changes over the past few months, which have left Logan and me worrying. The brooding dark-haired guy in expensive clothing trailing her is one of Logan's biggest concerns when it comes to Nikki's strange, new behavior.

"Hey, Max," I say, still uneasy from his appearance in my dream. Misplaced or not.

"Happy natal day," Max says.

I blink and then smile, but Logan rolls his eyes.

"Hey," I say to Logan when he wraps his broad arms around me, pulling me in for one of his famous, all-encompassing hugs. His familiar woodsy scent nestles around me.

"Happy birthday, Rena. Sorry. My, uh, dad couldn't make it," he says to Aunt Odette, who waves it off.

"One Andrews is plenty, and you're my favorite of the lot," she teases, knowing as well as I do how much it hurts Logan that his dad is such a workaholic. Mr. Andrews owns a contracting firm that builds cabins for anyone, from the professional mountain man to the tourist who just wants to build a summer home. He has allowed work to become his new wife in the wake of Logan's mom's death a few years back.

"Thanks for coming," I say, extricating myself from the awkwardly long hug.

Logan grins and slowly releases his hold. His gray eyes sparkle down on me, and he runs a hand through his sandy-blond hair.

Nikki's parents, Aunt Brynna and Uncle Christian, emerge from the kitchen with Simon Turner, the only person on the Alverson property who can cook worth a damn and the chef of the business.

Aunt Odette went to high school with Nikki's mom and dad. She and Aunt Brynna grew up together and have been best friends as far back as they can remember. Hence the whole "aunt" and "uncle" thing.

I catch a whiff of the dish that Simon carries, and my stomach rumbles.

"I even surprised myself with this one. Vegan ratatouille, for our little humanitarian artist." He grins.

"She's not so little anymore, Simon," Aunt Brynna teases.

Aunt Odette sighs, and Aunt Brynna squeezes her lightly around the shoulder.

"Just think, they're us, basically yesterday," Aunt Odette says, staring at me and Nikki.

Nikki snorts. "Yeah, if yesterday was 1972."

Aunt Brynna raises an eyebrow. "Actually, we were 90s kids, brat." We laugh, but I can't tell if Aunt Brynna was just teasing Nikki, or if she meant to be nastier with that word choice.

Aunt Odette eyes the two of us with a smile. "It's weird, looking at them, isn't it?" she says to Aunt Brynna. "Like looking at old pictures of ourselves." She flashes a wistful smile.

"Pfft, they're the knock-off us," Aunt Brynna says. They both dissolve into peals of laughter.

Simon hands them fresh glasses of white wine. "Well, at least they are entertaining," he says to Uncle Christian, nodding toward my two aunts.

Uncle Christian chuckles and then walks up to me.

"Happy birthday, Serena," he says, giving me a hug that Aunt Brynna and Aunt Odette both pile on top of.

"Simon, help!" I squeak.

From his place by the bar, Simon calls the adults over, pouring Uncle Christian a beer, and already refilling Aunt Brynna's and Aunt Odette's glasses of wine that they somehow managed to suck down.

"Man, do you think we will be total lushes like that in our forties?" Nikki says, a little too loudly. "I mean, what else is there to do in the mountains?"

"Nikkola!" Aunt Brynna scolds, glaring over her shoulder. In all fairness, the only time Aunt Odette drinks is when Aunt Brynna comes over. But Aunt Brynna has earned her wino title.

"Not in our forties yet," Aunt Odette calls over her shoulder, before turning back to whatever she and Simon are discussing.

"Hey, beer wench!" Nikki calls to Simon. "I made Serena a birthday playlist. Hook my phone up to the sound system?"

"Depends what's on it." Simon folds his arms across his chest, an unlikely indie-snob-banter-bond existing between them.

"LCD Soundsystem, Belle and Sebastian, Mitski, The Rapture . . ."

"Yes, yes, yes, no."

"Simon . . ." I pout.

"Fine." He accepts Nikki's phone and syncs her music to the speakers. She grins. "You're a gentleman and a scholar. So . . . what do you want to do first, Serena? Open your presents! I can't wait to give you ours. I almost ruined it eleventy times today alone!"

"Yes!" I grin back.

"Nikkola, that's after dinner," Aunt Brynna calls back.

"Her sense of hearing is annoyingly far-reaching," Nikki mutters.

"Oh, what does it matter, Brynna? If Serena wants to open presents, let her," Uncle Christian says.

"Yeah, the food has to cool a little anyway," Simon offers.

"Okay, ours first!" Nikki claps her hands together. I can feel her mother's eyes on her and glance in her direction.

Sure enough, Aunt Brynna glares daggers. *What the heck?* Nikki isn't even doing anything. Thankfully, Nikki doesn't seem to notice. It's not the first time that her overbearing mom has come down on her hard while drinking.

Nikki hands me a lavender gift bag. I look at my present pile and smile because everything is lavender.

"Man, you guys have my number, huh?" I joke.

The adults laugh, and my friends and Lena grin at me. Laurel is consumed by whatever is on her phone.

Nikki shoves the gift bag in my face. I reach in, and crushed velvet melts into my hands as I pull out a hunter-green vintage Fendi hobo bag, without one drop of leather on it. Charcoal beads stipple the front and back.

"Oh, Nik! How in the world?" There's no way she makes enough to buy this purse, waiting tables here for Aunt Odette and Simon part time.

Max grins, and I have my answer.

"Callie helped locate it. Wasn't easy, since Fendi is known for leather," Nikki says.

Inner conflict wrinkles my nose, because I refuse to own anything that means an animal died for me to have it.

"Callie and I even made sure that the freaking velvet and the satin lining came from vegan sources. Let me tell you how fun that was. I swear, not one creature died in the making of this bag." Nikki reassures me.

"Except for a hippie's bell bottoms," Simon cracks.

"Nikki, this is too much!" I gasp, twirling it around in my hand, and then standing to admire it on my arm.

"My best friend only turns eighteen once. Plus, Callie was really cool about it. She said it's the one piece that has entered her shop that she knows with one-hundred-percent certainty you won't . . . 'defile'? I believe that was the word she chose."

Aw, Callie. I make a mental note to not hack any vintage finds from her consignment shop for at least a few weeks.

"She even let me make payments. Max offered to pay for the whole thing, but that's not how I roll." Nikki winks.

"I love it." I breathe out, still admiring it. All the planning Nikki clearly put into the gift chokes me up.

"Open the inside pocket!" she says.

"But—" I object, because there had better not be anything else.

Four xx tickets slip into my hands.

I glance up, and Uncle Christian and Aunt Brynna raise their glasses, acknowledging their contribution to my amazing gift.

"The xx?" I shriek. "NO WAY!"

They have sold out the past couple of times Nikki and I have tried to see them in Red Rocks.

"Happy birthday, kiddo!" Uncle Christian calls.

"Happy birthday to all of us!" Nikki grins, pulling me up to dance around in circles with her, Max, and the tickets. Logan steps to the side, but still smiles, holding a hand out to spin Nikki.

I set the tickets and purse down so I can hug her and awkwardly hug Max, all the while feeling guilty for my weird dream involving him. Then I head over to Uncle Christian and Aunt Brynna and hug them, too.

"You do have more presents over there." Aunt Odette winks, taking a sip from her glass.

"I'll go put the food back in the oven, because I'm guessing it's cooler than we want." Simon heads toward the table to check on it.

"Sorry!" I call after him, but he waves me off, laidback as ever.

When I head back over to my present pile, I unwrap a beautiful crystal bracelet from Logan, with matching earrings.

"Oh, wow—this is gorgeous. Thank you!" I say. He wraps me in another of those hugs that are starting to feel less friendly and more like something else, so I clear my throat and step back.

Simon's gifts are quite predictable. Two new PlayStation games, because I am the only one who plays with him.

"Are these for me or you?" I ask, holding them up, and he laughs.

"Open mine next," Laurel demands. And since it's weird for her to openly participate in anything these days, I go along with it.

Nikki hands me a lavender box. I open the lid and then narrow my eyes when I pull out the vintage Ramones shirt that *I* bought from Callie's Consignments and spent close to five hours hacking the back of so that I could weave glass beads into it. Of course, I had to hide this from Callie, because she considers my vintage clothing hacks to basically be sacrilege.

I stand up, letting the box fall from my lap, the shirt in my hands.

"Are you *kidding* me? My Ramones shirt!"

I have been searching for it since August. I wanted to wear it on the first day of school and had accused Laurel of stealing it. I even got in trouble, because I had gone after her, and Aunt Odette didn't find the shirt in her room.

Nikki snorts and then covers her mouth, forcing a straight face.

"What?" Laurel demands. "I wanted to give you something I knew you would love."

"Hey, twisted little ray of sunshine," Aunt Odette says to Laurel from the bar. "You and I are talking later."

"Here, open mine?" Lena asks, handing me a large gift bag. "It's actually from Laurel, too."

"Is not," Laurel grumbles.

I pat Lena's hand, because she is forever the peacemaker of the house. I open the bag and find the three-hundred-count Prismacolor pencil set I have been drooling over, along with a portable easel and three sketchpads, all with different types of paper.

"Lena!" I say in shock.

"Check out the easel." Simon points the bottleneck in his hand toward it. "She spent hours at my place painting it for you, so you wouldn't see it."

I pull the easel from the bag. The cherry wood has been covered in cherry blossom branches, with petals falling.

"Oh, Bug. This is amazing." I set it down and pull my youngest sister in so I can give her a squeeze, her face beet-red.

Lena mumbles, "Just wanted to give you something you can hang on to."

"It's perfect," I say.

"Yeah, just like *she* is," Laurel mutters.

Lena's eyes glisten, and she looks away.

"Aaaaaaaaand later is now. Kitchen," Aunt Odette says.

"Big surprise," Laurel snaps, stomping through the dining area to follow our aunt.

Simon sighs. I hug Lena and whisper encouragement that I know falls on deaf ears.

Before hormones, Laurel was one of my favorite people to spend time with. Now, not so much.

One present sits in the once-full pile. A lavender envelope with Aunt Odette's handwriting. She is still in the kitchen, her voice raising as she tries to talk sense into my sister, so I place it in the back pocket of my jeans.

Logan touches my shoulder. "Hey, can I talk to you for a second?"

My throat tightens, because I'm not ready to talk about what I think he wants to discuss. I nod anyway.

Logan leads the way to the patio door. Nikki waggles her eyebrows at us as we walk by. I narrow my eyes at her.

Logan holds the door open for me. The globe lights that Simon strung on the wooden railings and the metal awning cast a hazy glow over the mist coming off Havenwood Falls.

I walk to the railing and glance down at the waterfall that the patio overlooks. I have often wondered if this was the best location for a bar patio.

The roar of the water sends a chill through my spine, reminding me of my dream, and I shiver violently.

"You cold?" Logan asks, shrugging out of his red flannel shirt before I can answer.

I nod, and he helps me slip my arms into it.

"Thanks, but now aren't you cold?" I ask, gesturing toward his black T-shirt.

"The way Coach had us running laps after bombing out last week, I think I'll be toasty all winter," he jokes, referring to their big loss, which wiped out all chances of a homecoming game.

"So, uh, thanks for my gift," I say, glancing down at the charcoal crystals that glitter on my wrist. I realize that it's the exact same shade as the beads on my purse, which is still on my arm, because I am in love.

He smiles. "Nikki and I coordinated."

"I'm so lucky. I really do have the best best-friends a girl could ask for."

He winces a little, and I clear my throat. It feels like ever since we became seniors, Logan and I have fallen out of sync.

"Speaking of Nikki . . ." Logan says. "That's why I asked you out here."

"Oh?" I try to cover the relief in my voice, but I am almost positive I fail.

He hesitates for a moment. "Yeah, I still think Max is giving her drugs of some sort."

"I don't know, Logan. Max seems really nice."

"Why is everyone so blind? Nikki is clearly exhibiting classic signs of drug use, ever since dating him. Drastic change in appearance, ditching school, and she's mean all the time," he says.

"I just feel like if it were the case, I would *know*."

"Oh, are you 'psychic' like she is, too?" He rolls his eyes. As kids, Nikki always teased us that she was a witch. In middle school, that switched to botched fortune telling.

"I won't argue some of those points. Something is definitely going on, but I just don't get that vibe from Max like you do."

"Is it because he bought you an expensive purse?" Logan snaps.

"Um, wow. No," I answer in the same frosty tone.

He sighs and scrubs his hair with both hands. "I'm sorry. That was stupid."

"Yeah, it was." I bump his shoulder with mine. "But I know you meant well. You care about her. I get it."

"Well, talk to her or something, please?" He asks. "Nik and I are in such a weird place ever since that douchenozzle came to town. She doesn't really talk to me or hang out anymore, like it bothers him or something."

"And you're so welcoming and friendly to Max. It's mind-boggling, really!" I tease.

He mutters something under his breath.

"I'll tell you what. I'll work on talking to Nikki, but can you please work on being open to Max? You could be wrong about him. Plus, it will make her happy if we can all be friends."

"The hell does she care what I think?" He mumbles.

I cock my head to the side and flash him a *duh* look. "You know you've always been a sort of big brother figure to her. When she picks on you, it's because she feels like you don't approve of her anymore. She's hurt, so she lashes out at you."

"She has changed so much. I don't even know if I would be friends with this Nikki if we had just met," he grumbles.

"Well, that's not the case. She's always been there for us, Logan. A few years ago, did she leave you hanging when you needed her most?"

Logan looks away. I know bringing up his mom's death was a low blow, but he's so stubborn that I have to get through to him any way I can.

He sighs, and I know I have won. "Why do you girls have to be so damn complicated?"

I snort. "Yeah, *we* are the complicated ones. Reasons why I have basically always been single."

He mumbles something else.

"What?" I ask.

"Nothing. Look, we should head back in." He gestures toward the table that Simon and the other adults are busy filling with food.

"Wait." I grab Logan's wrist as he turns away.

He slowly turns to face me, his eyes sad.

"No matter what happens this year, the three of us stick together. Right? If it's drugs, we deal with it and help her. If it's her psychotic mother, which is more likely the case, we deal with it and help her."

Logan glares at me. "And if it's the douche canoe from New York, *I* will deal with it."

"Logan," I sigh.

He grins, dimples appearing. "I said I would try to get along with him, but I didn't agree to starting tonight."

Logan winks and then takes my hand and leads me inside.

CHAPTER 2

*W*e all sit back in our chairs, stuffed with vegan ratatouille, French bread, various salads, and multiple French side dishes that Simon slaved over in preparation for my birthday dinner.

"Seriously, the best meal I have had in weeks," Logan says.

"Ha!" I shoot up in triumph, digging for my phone.

"What are you doing?" Logan asks.

"Wait." I set my voice recorder and then lean over the table so I am directly in front of him. "Please repeat what you said about a vegan dinner being amazing."

He snorts and bats my hand away. "Dork."

"Nerd," I fire back.

"Good God, get a room already," Laurel whines.

"Laurel!" Aunt Odette snaps, her cheeks rosy from the wine. "Apologize."

"So sorry." She rolls her eyes and then walks out of the tavern, toward the house.

"Laurel!" Aunt Odette calls after her.

"Let her go, Odette," Simon coaxes. "She needs to cool down."

Aunt Odette sighs. "I just don't understand what I am doing wrong with her."

Aunt Brynna leans against her, wrapping a bangle-clad arm around

Aunt Odette's shoulders. "Nothing. It's not you. It's the age." She gestures toward Nikki when she says it.

Nikki's fork clatters onto her plate. "That's right, Brynna. Deflect that blame right back on the growing teen instead of the lies and pressure being placed on her by the parents."

"Nikki! That's enough," Uncle Christian thunders. I stop mid-chew. Uncle Christian never yells, but he probably spoke up because both of my aunts are still trying to remove their jaws from the table.

Nikki picks her fork back up and continues picking at the remaining food on her plate, like nothing happened.

"Apologize, right now," Uncle Christian continues.

"Aunt O, that wasn't meant for you, entirely, sorry. Brynna . . . nope," Nikki says, popping the *p* and then taking a bite of a roll while smirking at her mother.

Uncle Christian slides his chair back to stand, but Aunt Brynna shakes her head, never removing her eyes from her daughter.

"Christian, it's fine. Leave it. Nikkola, we will discuss this at home."

"Once the rosé is on ice, I'm sure," Nikki fires back.

An awkward silence settles over the room. Logan and I meet eyes, and he shakes his head, as if to say, "See?"

I try to catch Nikki's attention, but she won't look at me.

"Hey, I want to see this fabulous cake of yours, Odette." Simon's voice takes on a strained pitch, probably trying to distract everyone.

A smile brightens her face. "Ooh! Yes!"

Aunt Odette leaps from the table, also overly eager to move on from the weirdness, it seems. She returns with a four-tiered chocolate cake that looks like it could be from a wedding magazine.

"Aunt Odette!" My jaw hits the table. "How?"

"I've been practicing on slow days," she says, sticking candles in the cake.

Once they are lit, Simon dims the lights, and everyone sings. I smile through teary eyes, thinking of my mama's missing face, in addition to Laurel's.

I look up, and everyone stares at me.

Aunt Odette drapes her arms around me. "You should probably decide on a wish and blow them out before we eat wax, sweetheart."

"I know, it's just . . . I wish Mama had been well enough to be here," I whisper.

Aunt Odette sighs. "Honey, Margot is here in spirit, along with your father and others we have lost. I firmly believe that. But I do wish they were all here in person, too." She squeezes me.

I close my eyes to make the one wish I have always wanted—for my family to be complete again. For Mama to find a way to climb out of the mental prison she has been locked away in since Daddy died.

My candles flicker out, and everyone claps.

"Okay, drumroll!" Simon commands.

Aunt Odette shakes her head at him but grins as she slices into my beautiful cake.

And then it implodes.

Sticky goo runs all over the lavender lace table cloth, an erupting volcano of cake.

"Oh, crap!" Aunt Odette cries.

Aunt Brynna jumps up and runs into the kitchen to retrieve towels so we can help Aunt Odette mop it up.

"I cooked that sucker for hours!" Aunt Odette wails. "Serena, I am so sorry."

Everyone looks at me, wide-eyed, gauging my reaction.

Laughter rips through my body—painfully, given how full I am. A snort or two later, everyone joins in, tears running down some of their faces.

"I will never be able to cook," Aunt Odette hoots between gasps of air.

"Well, that's why you have me." Simon's eyes crinkle with amusement as he walks out of the kitchen. He'd managed to slip away unnoticed while we were all in hysterics.

In his arms is a less impressive, but hopefully cooked, two-layer cake with cream frosting and lavender pearl candies around the edges.

"I really wanted to support you, Odette. But, I also know you, so I ordered this from Health Nut weeks ago." Simon explains, referring to the health food store in town, owned by Stella Daryn, the mom of one of my classmates, Ellisyn.

"My hero." Aunt Odette winks at him, and my eyebrows raise. Has she finally figured out how perfect he is for her?

"Yeah, a regular knight in shining armor," Simon teases. He and Aunt Odette laugh so hard over that one that she snorts.

"I don't get how it's that funny," I say, one corner of my mouth poking up in reaction to them.

Aunt Odette waves me away, like it's an inside joke or something.

"Vegan carrot cake with cream cheese frosting, made from cashews. A little bird told me it's your favorite." Simon places it in front of me.

"Uh . . . I think I'll take my chances with Odette's cake." Logan winces at the smaller cake and Uncle Christian chuckles.

Simon opens a second package of candles.

"No, don't sing again, please." I blush, not wanting all the attention.

He nods, cutting and serving the cake instead.

I shift in my seat, and something digs into my back. "Ow!"

I glance behind me and pull Aunt Odette's gift from my back pocket.

"Oh, yay! Open!" she demands.

I take a couple of bites of the delicious cake first, trying to rein in my response to how good it is, not wanting to hurt my aunt's feelings. Then I tear the envelope open.

A card with a woman carrying a sleeping little girl, the girl's head on the woman's shoulder, is on the front. The woman faces the ocean, as the sun beats down.

The inside is blank, save for a scrawled note that says:

YOU WILL ALWAYS BE our baby.
Even if you're too big to carry.
Happy 18th!
Love,
Aunt Odette and Mama

Two round-trip airline tickets to Paris fall out.

"Aunt Odette!" I gasp.

She grins. "I know you have been saving, but I wanted to do this for you."

I jump up from the table and crush her in a bear hug. My plans for a gap year, before finding a university somewhere overseas, and then studying art, haven't always been met with such enthusiasm from her. She squeezes me, and I settle back into my chair, looking at the tickets. I note the departure and arrival dates and have the reason for her excitement right in front of me.

"This is a two-week trip?" I ask.

Her smile falls into a straight line. "Yes, so you can sightsee with Nikki and explore, and then come back to start at a community school closer to home."

"But, I'm not coming back. Remember?" My mouth dries. "I have been saving for this for years. I am taking a year off and traveling. Then I will figure out what art school I want to attend, once I know for sure which country I want to stay in."

"Serena, I'm sorry, but that cannot happen," my aunt says.

"Brynna isn't allowing my Seattle plans, either," Nikki says shortly.

Aunt Brynna's eyes flash at Nikki.

Nikki continues, "Too bad for them that we are adults at eighteen, huh?"

"Nikkola, not another word," Aunt Brynna warns through clenched teeth.

Nikki glares at her.

My hands shake as I place the tickets on the table. Nikki is right. I am an adult now, well, in theory at least. As soon as I graduate, I am free to do what I want. I stand.

"Aunt Odette, thank you for this party, but no thank you for the gift. If they are nonrefundable tickets, I will pay you back from my savings."

Everyone quiets down, and I look around the room. "Thank you, everyone. For coming, and for the gifts. It was wonderful . . ."

I run from the tavern to the house before my tears of frustration fall.

~

Someone knocks on my bedroom door.

"May I please come in?" Aunt Odette asks.

I grunt in response, brushing my hair as I stand in front of my dresser mirror.

Aunt Odette comes up behind me and wraps her arms around my waist.

"I know you are mad about college, but can you please just trust that I am trying to look out for you? What if you don't get in anywhere in Europe? College is super competitive as it is, but internationally? Plus, what if this whole gap year idea of yours messes up your chances?"

My nostrils flare, and she hugs me tighter.

"That came out wrong. You are more talented than anyone else I know, and I believe that you can and will do amazing things. But I am also being realistic. We don't know what is going on with your mother's condition. I don't want to burden you with it, but would you want to be far if we needed you home, quickly? Why not take some basic college courses online, or locally, to start?"

"No," I whisper.

"Look, my gift still stands. Two full weeks abroad with Nikki, after graduation. God help me and my nerves. Brynna, Christian, and I will cover the entire thing, but you *will* return home two weeks later. You just . . .you have to." Her voice cracks.

I whirl on her in defiance. "Why? Will I turn into a pumpkin? Or will you just disown me if you lose control over my life?"

She takes a deep breath. "Let's make a deal. I will explain more to you before you leave. Can you just trust that I will tell you everything that you need to know, as you need to know it?"

"Cryptic much?"

"Serena . . ." she pleads.

I sigh. "Okay, fine. But secrets don't make friends."

Her shoulders sag. Guilt tugs at the loose strands of my anger, unraveling it some.

"Friends also do not bake cakes for friends if they are terrible at it." I attempt a light tone.

She snorts, and then laughs out loud. "God, it was awful. The sad thing is I really tried."

I lean over and kiss her cheek. "You know I don't care about that. And I do appreciate the thought behind it."

I glance at our reflection in my dresser mirror. Passersby in town often mistake us for sisters, and it's no surprise. I favor her features more than my own mama's.

She sighs and plays with my hair. "I cannot believe you're eighteen. I feel like only yesterday you were this pink little bundle of yumminess."

"Wasn't I cross-eyed?" I ask, wrinkling my nose.

"You outgrew it, and you were still the prettiest baby. So, now for the heavy. I have another present for you."

She turns me around and leads us over to sit on the edge of my bed.

"Aw, Aunt Odette, really—it's not necessary."

"Hush."

"It's not food, is it?" I wince, and she laughs.

"I am trying for a moment here between us!" she says, pulling a tiny box, wrapped in lavender paper with a tiny silver bow, from the pocket of her oversized cardigan.

"The last Alverson to wear this necklace that I am about to give you was your aunt Karina."

She deposits the box into my hands. I sit on the edge of my bed and slip a finger under the seam, sliding it through the tape. The paper falls right off, revealing a sapphire blue velvet box.

I glance up at her, and she waves me on to continue, her iPhone at the ready to snap pictures, blinding me with the flash as I pout my way through.

"Is that really necessary?"

"It's a momentous occasion. One day, you will be glad that I took all these pictures."

The box creaks open and reveals a delicate, but upon inspection strong, silver chain. The silver claw setting weaves into an intricate design, cradling a clear crystal with bubbles within it that move around as I rotate the charm in my hand.

"Here, let me help you," she offers, opening the clasp and draping it over my neck.

I hold the crystal of the necklace in my fingers, pulling the silver chain up from my neck. It looks like a geode—rather ugly, save for the bubbles inside the crystal that glitter and sparkle, catching the light.

Feeling Aunt Odette's eyes on me, I glance up. She stares at me expectantly, and I clear my throat.

"Oh! It's really . . . unique." I offer.

She smiles at it in quiet adoration before saying, "I know it's not the most beautiful thing to look at. Some of the more important things in life are the plainest. Every Alverson woman has worn this necklace. Your great-great-great-great-aunt Josie wore it when she traveled to Havenwood Falls by covered wagon with her sisters and her father, your great-great . . ."

"I get it," I interject with a grin.

"Grandfather, Jedidiah," she finally finishes. "Your aunt Karina was the last Alverson woman to wear it before she . . ."

Aunt Odette doesn't like to talk about her baby sister, who died as a teenager, aside from Aunt Karina's birthday each August, when we picnic on her grave, in her memory.

"Aunt Odette!" Laurel calls from downstairs. From her tone, she is clearly over the mood she was in at dinner. "Beulah and Esmerelda ripped the trash apart again! They must have been here earlier."

Aunt Odette groans. "Damn bears. I need a shotgun and a shovel."

"Don't you dare!" I jump to my feet in protection of the black bears, whose curiosity far outweighs their fear of people. From the time she was a cub, Beulah, as we named her, has been a constant presence on our land. Much to my aunt's chagrin, Beulah showed up with a cub in tow this spring. They are basically the closest thing to pets that my sisters and I have.

"Don't worry. Since it's dark, I'm sure she's long gone and safe for the moment."

"You mean, safe forever." I try.

Aunt Odette stands, gathering the crumpled wrapping paper from my bed. "No one is safe for that long 'round these parts." Her voice is light but something strange flickers in her eyes.

She pivots at the door. "Hey—are you feeling okay? I know you said that you had a bad dream, but you looked flushed when you woke up. Do you feel sick—or different?"

She eyes me strangely, her view dashing down to the necklace momentarily before meeting my eyes once more.

I sigh. "I haven't gotten my, *you know*, if that's your down-low way of asking," I mutter, referring to the fact that I am now an eighteen-year-old who *still* doesn't have her period.

She clears her throat. "Well, don't worry, honey. The doctors aren't concerned, so we shouldn't be either. I am sorry to bring it up. I only asked because I have strange dreams and nightmares sometimes before I get mine. So, I thought maybe . . ."

"Ugh." I cover my ears. "Don't really want to know."

She winks and then blows me a kiss, before disappearing into the hallway. Her voice echoes, carrying on about bear stew, bearskin boots, and other things that make my little vegan heart shrivel up and die.

My eyes travel down my dresser, to the picture of me, Mama, and Daddy, taken the day I was born. My throat tightens, and the urge to see her spurns my feet toward the hallway leading to the third-floor home of our own Miss Havisham.

Mama's thin, white-washed planked door stands open, probably to let some air in. It gets hot on the third floor, but Mama doesn't tolerate the central air, so we mostly leave it off up there to keep her content.

The same song that she has listened to nonstop on Daddy's old record player, since the day he died, echoes eerily down the stairs, filling the hallway. A breeze wisps through the open window at the foot of Mama's stairs, the curtain a phantom in a somber dance to the music.

"Mama?" My voice bounces off the log walls, and my bare feet pad against the wide-planked wooden floating stairs.

No answer, other than the steady creaking that I know to be her rocking chair. This is normal, so I sigh and keep going, lowering my head at the stair landing to account for the pendant light fixture. It was added to the hardwood ceiling molding during one of the many updates each generation of Alversons has made to keep our cabin going over the past couple of centuries.

With a deep breath, I steel myself against Mama's ripe stench, growing with each step I take into her room. She used to allow us to bathe her once or twice a week, but now her aquaphobia has worsened to the point that it's almost impossible to make her go near water, except for little fluke instances when she doesn't fight it. The air flowing in through the open window in her bedroom jettisons off the cross breeze from the stairwell, making it slightly more bearable.

"Mama?" I ask again, with less resolve this time. I don't know what I expect her to say or do. I've long ago given up on getting a response.

I vaguely remember the start of it all, when Daddy died the summer before I began kindergarten. Mama slowly slipped into fits where nobody could reach her. She would just sit in this room and stare at their wedding picture, like she's doing right now. But it would come and go. Catatonic, they called it. Aunt Odette gave up the small room attached to the tavern, where Simon now lives, and moved into the main house to help her. But Mama still slid deeper into her darkness, until she never left the room again, unassisted.

"So, it's my birthday. Eighteen! I'm finally old enough to vote, buy a pack of cigarettes, and buy a gun without parental consent." I sink down onto the edge of her bed and snort. "I mean, we both know I will only be doing one of those things."

My smile fades. Nothing. The familiar urgency to connect with this woman who brought me into the world swirls up.

"Mama—I . . . I wish you had been at dinner. Aunt Odette tried to bake me a cake, and it was totally raw in the middle. Good thing Simon predicted that one and ordered a backup."

I glance down and trace my fingers over the strange crystal on my neck. "And then Aunt Odette gave me this necklace . . . she said it was Aunt Karina's and is an heirloom or something. I feel bad, because I think it's sort of ugly, but it seems like it means a lot to her for me to wear it."

The silence of the room catches my attention, so I trail off and look up at Mama. No longer rocking, she sits in her chair, still as stone. Slowly, she glances up and over at me, as if shaking off a dream.

"Mama?" I ask, voice breaking, my hope a pathetic zombie.

Maybe this is it.

"Mama? Please come back to us," I plead, moving toward her, grabbing her hand, but she wrenches it away from me and jabs her pointer finger at . . . my necklace?

"What is it? Do you want this? I'm sorry! You can have it." I move to unclasp the necklace, and it all happens so fast.

Mama stands, one hand clawing at my necklace as I gasp and back away. Then she grabs a framed picture of her, Aunt Karina, and Aunt Odette as teenagers from the table, and flings it at me. I gasp and jump out of the way as it crashes into the framed wedding picture on the wall behind me, spider-webbing Daddy's handsome face.

"Oh, God, no. Mama, I'm so sorry!"

She falls to the floor, sobbing, her eyes on me in accusation.

Footsteps pound the stairs behind me, and Aunt Odette lifts Mama into her chair, as Mama kicks and punches, crying and screaming.

"Here, let me help." I move toward them.

Mama shrieks.

"No! Serena, give her some room," Aunt Odette pleads.

Mama lurches toward the window, almost bumping her head on the angled ceiling, but Aunt Odette deflects the blow onto her own arm instead. Forever protecting her big sister.

"For heaven's sake!" Aunt Odette cries out, shaking her arm and wincing as the twins run into the room. "Serena, please, love, just go. It will be okay."

"What the hell did you *do*?" Laurel rushes to Aunt Odette's aid.

"I didn't—I don't know . . . I showed her my necklace, and she freaked out."

Something dark passes over Aunt Odette's face, and then she waves Laurel off and leans into Mama, whispering in her ear.

Mama's body goes slack. She stops punching Aunt Odette, collapsing into her arms in muted tears.

Laurel glares at me.

Lena yanks me from the room, dragging me back down the third-floor stairs. Once we are in the hall, Mama's screams reverberating through us, Lena threads her thin fingers through mine.

"S'not your fault," she mumbles.

"No, it is. She was fine until I went in."

"Who's to say she wouldn't have had the episode regardless? Maybe it's that new medication Aunt Odette has been talking about that the doctor gave Mama last time."

I smile sadly at my little sister and tuck a stray blond wisp behind her ear. "I love you for this, but it's not your job to make me feel better, or to take care of me. That's my job with *you*."

She frowns. "I like to think it's equal. That the three of us look out for each other."

I smile. "You're a wise little Bug, but I'm fine."

"Serena, you're shaking . . ." she continues, reaching out for my hand, but I step back.

"Really, I'm fine," I say in a firmer tone. "I just want to go think."

I slip down the stairs and out the front door before Lena can say anything else. To the far left, behind our makeshift garage that was added centuries after the cabin was built, I can still see remnants of Beulah and Esmerelda's buffet.

Aunt Odette must've called it quits for the night, which is a blessing. I don't feel like any more talks or inquisitions.

I crave the roaring quiet and peace that only one place can provide. My heart gallops when I kick my shoes off and dip my toes into the small body of water that couldn't decide between forming as a small lake or a large pond.

I feel stupid that a dream has me dipping a toe in trepidation, but it was so real.

Not even thinking, I step in, clothes and all, wading up to my shoulders in the warm water. Aunt Odette says that it is secretly fed by a hot spring, and it's like a lukewarm hot tub without the maintenance. The heat is inviting against the chilly air. With a deep breath I go under, my mind wrestling with the image of me pulling myself in, from my dream—probably nothing more than a weird Freudism about senior year and finding myself or whatever.

Something sears against my chest, and I gasp. Forgetting I am underwater, I suck in a lungful and propel myself to the surface.

Spluttering and hacking, I struggle to clear my airway, and then I open my eyes. The scent of burning flesh registers in the background as the water takes on that weird green backlight from below, like in my dream.

I claw at the necklace, and when I move it from my chest, there is a burn mark in its wake. I open my mouth to scream, but nothing comes out other than a squeak, as the crystal lights up in my hand.

Brilliant colors of the rainbow color my flesh, strobing onto the still water.

As quickly as it began, it stops. I glance up and see shadows against the mouth of the lagoon that peeks out in between strips of the waterfall. That's when I find my voice and yelp, attempting to swim backwards out of the water.

When my feet hit the shore, I glance up at my cabin. Mama's window calls to me. I don't know why. Just like conversations with Mama, it's usually dark and empty. But something white flickers there. I blink and look closer.

Mama stands in the window, staring directly at me, but that's impossible. Even when she had her episode earlier, she couldn't stand alone. Yet, there she is, eyes wide, mouth wide and gaping in a silent scream. A chill threads itself along my spine. I blink, and Mama's gone. I glance away and look back again, clearing my view, just to be sure.

Still nothing. Just a vacuous black hole.

CHAPTER 3

*I*n the comforting light of day, the strange happenings of last night feel like nothing more than a crazy dream. The events and questions tug at me, demanding answers. Yet I know that after our spat about going away to school last night, the last thing to help my case will be Aunt Odette thinking I am delusional.

I make my way down the stairs and look over the banister, searching for the twins. They are both on the couch, predictable as ever —Lena buried in a textbook, while Laurel cracks her gum, FaceTiming her friend, Alicia.

"What could you two possibly have to talk about at this hour?" I ask in exasperation. "You're going to see her at school in like five minutes."

Laurel rolls her eyes at me and turns over on her side on the couch, hiding behind a curtain of white-blond. She lowers her voice to a grumble and then they both shriek with laughter.

I nudge Lena. "You know you're my favorite, right?"

She flashes a sly smile as I slip into the kitchen and swipe a travel mug from the cupboard, filling it with black coffee. I grab an apple from the bowl on the table and then scoop the keys to the Jeep up with my other hand.

Aunt Odette looks up from emptying the dishwasher and smiles at me. "Hey, were you night-swimming?"

"Uhh . . ."

"Why?" Her eyes pierce me, and it feels like anything I say here is critical.

"I just needed air, after Mama," I answer.

Her eyes flit down. Score one for me.

"How is she?" I ask.

"Better, but I am going to run it by her doctor today."

I bite my lip, guilt washing over me again.

"The only thing you need to be flashing those guilty puppy-dog eyes over is sneaking out on a school night and then dripping all over the floor. Don't do it again."

"Sorry," I mumble.

She comes up to me and cups my face. "I have to be strict sometimes, but please know I am here if you want to talk." She gives me that same expectant look that she did last night.

As much as I want to ask her more about the necklace, my gut tells me that if I let on that I could potentially be crazy, I will have to kiss Europe goodbye, permanently.

"Serena," she says with a look on her face as if she might be repeating herself to get my attention.

"What? Sorry."

"You okay?"

"Yeah," I lie.

"Okay. Don't forget to hand your excuse in to the office so you can come home early to set up for Harvest," Aunt Odette says, handing me three sheets of paper. One each for Lena, Laurel, and me.

"Wait, *what?*"

Aunt Odette blinks. "The Carnival at the Falls. I need you girls home early to help with setup."

"No, you said, 'Harvest,'" I argue.

She hesitates for a minute and then sighs. "Honey, I am exhausted. I haven't had coffee yet. It's fall. Harvest is pretty much always the theme." She suddenly becomes busy, organizing papers on the table, and no longer meeting my eyes.

Are we both keeping secrets now?

I stare her down for a minute longer and then call over my shoulder, "Lena. Laurel. In the Jeep now, or you're walking."

A growl comes from the living room, and then Laurel stomps out.

"What's your problem now?" I ask, holding the door open for my sisters, with Aunt Odette trailing us.

Lena moves to the side to let her darker half pass. Aunt Odette tries to kiss Laurel's cheek, but Laurel ducks out of the way, as Lena steps in to accept it.

"Turner freaking asked Emily to homecoming," Laurel finally answers.

"You guys have been up for like twenty minutes. How is there already so much drama?"

Laurel mutters something darkly incoherent in response.

Aunt Odette mouths to me, "Have fun," and then pulls the screen door closed after us. I watch her figure recede up the mountain, toward the tavern to begin prepping for the afternoon shift and the busy night that the Carnival crowd will ensure.

I open the driver side door of the Jeep and sink into the seat, weary from a restless night without much sleep.

Laurel clicks away in the backseat, snorting and growling like a girl possessed with each *ping ping ping* of a text.

I glance at Lena in the passenger seat. "Thank you for beating her to shotgun," I say as I back up onto the dirt road that meets our driveway, rewarding myself with a sip of coffee.

"Alicia needs a ride," Laurel chirps when I turn onto the road opposite from the direction of her friend's house.

I groan because I just want to get to school and away from my sisters, so I can tell Nikki about everything that happened after she left my party and find out what the hell is going on between her and Aunt Brynna. I was tempted to call her last night or this morning, but it's not like that is info you can dump on someone over the phone.

"Laurel, we're gonna be late," Lena objects.

"Not with the way lead foot over here drives," Laurel says.

She's not wrong. Sheriff Kasun and Havenwood's finest are the bane of my driving existence. Yet, I still mutter under my breath, pull a U-turn, and drive five minutes out of the way to scoop up a giggling redhead. Her curls flounce like a cartoon character as she skips her way into the backseat.

"O. M. Geeeee! Emily totally just got grounded so Turner is up for grabs for homecoming!" Alicia announces.

Laurel squeals, and they do their weird little handshake-hair-flip.

"We should totally hit Aurelia up after school to go shopping!" Alicia says.

Lena buries herself deeper in her book and her seat. Last year, *she* was the twin Aurelia spent nearly every waking moment with, before moving on to hanging out with Laurel and her friends. I know it isn't fair, but witnessing Laurel leaving our sister out like that has left my patience waning.

I reach over and pat Lena's knee and then glance over my shoulder and mimic Laurel and her friend. "OMG! Maybe Turner will ask me! I'll find the pinkest, most glittery dress in existence, and count how many times he uses the word 'like' in a sentence the whole night."

Meeting their unimpressed glares, I turn around to back out of Alicia's driveway and onto the dirt road to retrace my steps toward Nikki's house.

"Seriously. Loser status, you freak," Laurel snaps.

"So, ReeRee . . ." Alicia tries out her newest nickname for me.

I mouth, "no," over my shoulder at her.

"How's that hottie, Logan?" Alicia asks, applying bubblegum-pink lipstick, using her cell phone as a mirror.

I choke on my coffee as she and Laurel cackle, shooting off more *ping ping pings*, and snorting in between.

For whatever reason, I find myself on the defensive. "He's too old for you. Wait—are you two seriously texting each other right now?"

They *ping* back and forth in response with the occasional "I know, right?" and "So lame."

I pull from the dirt road onto the pavement of Fifth Street, heading to Nikki's house on Seventh.

"Ugh. Why do we have to pick *her* up?" Alicia groans.

"It's my vehicle you're riding in, so, yeah. My friend."

"Actually, it's Aunt Odette's Jeep," Laurel interjects, always super happy to point that one out.

"Shut it," I mutter, pulling up to the gray clapboard Cape Cod with red shutters and wooden stars. Folk art punctuates the side of the house and the yard. Nikki's mom has a serious craft show obsession and will drive for miles just to find a new piece. We used to let her drag us along, just so we could get out of town for a day when we were younger.

Nikki slips out her screened front door, strutting her stuff in a very black, very mini skirt with fishnets and combat boots. One of the torn tee halters I made for her peeks through a jean jacket. I blink against a flashback of years past and all the pink she used to wear. Some of Logan's concerns are becoming impossible to ignore.

Nikki pulls her shades off and pops them into her cocoa hair, delicate nose wrinkling as she sees the shock of red.

"I'll get in the back," Lena says quickly.

Overhearing her, Nikki leans into her open window and winks. "No way, baby cakes. I'm always up for a backseat party."

My head hits my backrest, and I sigh.

Nikki and Alicia's feud is very real and undying, dating back to that one time Nikki babysat Alicia years ago. The little brat framed Nikki for stealing the mad money stash in her parents' safe, when really, Alicia took it herself to buy a billion Barbies and Pixy Stix. Even though Alicia's parents eventually discovered the truth and apologized, the damage was already done. Nikki was blacklisted from her short-lived babysitting career.

"Nancy," Alicia hisses, sliding away from Nikki, in a nod to the deranged goth girl from *The Craft*.

Nikki narrows her eyes and growls. "Weasley. Move your twig-butt over and pull the twig out while you're at it."

I back out of Nikki's driveway while she plugs her phone into the auxiliary jack, Soundgarden blaring as we pull into the Havenwood Falls High parking lot. I slow down, because nobody particularly pays attention or parks in any semblance of order. Kids sit on hoods of cars and hang out of windows, yelling at each other instead of making their way into the building.

"Let us out here?" Laurel asks, waving to Aurelia and their group of friends, leaning against the railing of the school's entrance.

I pull over so they can hop out, glancing at Lena, who remains buried in her book, clearly not wanting to join them.

"Leen?" Laurel asks.

I shake my head at her, and she sighs and then shuts the door behind Alicia after she hops out.

"Have a good day! Learn stuff!" Nikki calls after Laurel and her friend, Satan. Lena remains in her seat, paler than the paper in the book she reads.

"You okay, Bug?" I ask.

Lena nods unconvincingly.

"What is it?"

"Laurel's mad that I'm not going to homecoming," she mumbles. "But I don't see how it even matters. She has Alicia, and . . ."

"Aurelia?" I offer gently.

Lena looks down and blinks, whispering, "I don't know what I even did. I tried to be nice to Aurelia. I feel like something is so broken in me. I just cannot people."

Nikki pops her head between the front seats and nestles her cheek against Lena's in an awkward hug. "Oh, I can talk to Laurel for you. Aurelia, too." An odious grin consumes her face.

"Nik, no. Look, Lena, I know this probably doesn't help, but I can tell you that friends come and go and drift around at your age."

"You have had the same two best friends since kindergarten," Lena says with a glum sigh.

"Serena, Logan, and I are freaks of nature. Our friendship literally doesn't make sense. Worst case, I could always be your homecoming date." Nikki waggles her eyebrows. "Come on, we'll be the talk of the town. Irene will love it."

Irene Beckett is the town busybody, and that would probably give her gossip material for at least a full morning.

"You have Max." Lena sniffs, wiping the creases of her eyes before tears fully fall.

"Pfft. Boy can't dance to save his life. I would choose you first, any day," Nikki says.

"Bug, you know you are always welcome to come hang out with us," I echo. Lena smiles, but shakes her head. "Thanks, but no thanks."

"At least think about it?" I ask as we step out of the Jeep and grab our bags.

She shrugs and then heads off toward school. I sigh and lean back against the Jeep.

"Dude, I am seriously never having children," Nikki muses, so darkly that my gut tells me there might be more to her sentiment than my little sister drama.

"Tell me about it. I quite literally probably will not," I say, my health issues always in the back of my mind.

Nikki gives me a hug. "You don't know that. You and Logan will probably have a little army of mountain men."

I giggle.

"He will have his own football team," Nikki continues.

"Oh, stop. You know it's not like that between the two of us."

"But does *he*?" Nikki asks.

My cheeks burn, and the heat reminds me of what happened last night. The memory brings back the urgency to share it all with my best friend.

"Nikki, I really need to talk to you."

The five-minute warning bell blares across campus, so we head toward the building.

"So, let's leave," she says.

I stop in my tracks. "Uh . . . no. You have Ms. Bast first." She is a fun teacher, but one who will notice if you skip. "What the heck is going on with you, anyway? You never skipped school before and suddenly you just don't care?"

"Oh, you're overreacting," Nikki says as we walk up the stairs into the three-story brick building.

"Nik, you've missed three days this term alone. You cut your hair, like a lot. Your clothes, while interesting, are totally different . . ."

"What are you, my mom?" She snaps.

"Speaking of your mom, what the hell is going on with you two?"

"I'm quite sure I do not know what you're talking about." Nikki pulls the visor down and removes the sunglasses from her hair. Leaning into the mirror, she straightens some flyaways.

"Bullshit. What happened last night?"

She slams the visor back into place. "For the love of cheese, back off, Brynna Number Two."

I flinch, and Nikki sighs. "Look, I know you care, but I am seriously fine. I have spent my whole life doing what everyone wants and expects of me. This is senior year. Time to break free. Let's not take it so seriously, 'kay?"

I try to object, but she covers my mouth with her hand.

"I will release you if you promise we will only discuss *your* problems," Nikki says.

I nod and quickly tell her about my dream (minus the part about thinking Max abducted us) and the necklace as she opens her locker and takes out the books and folders needed for her morning classes.

"You guys are so cool with all your Old Family heirlooms and stories, unlike my boring family. And that dream is full of symbolism regarding all the stuff we are going through right now in senior year. Being in over our heads, loss of control, impending freedom."

"But, the necklace . . ." I insist.

Nikki picks the crystal up and examines it. "Could be more attractive," she ascertains.

"Nikki." I sigh.

"How many hours of sleep have you had this week?" she asks, worry knitting her brow.

"The same amount of time you've actually spent in class," I fire back.

She cocks her head to the side. "Maybe it's a combination of exhaustion and undercooked food?" She teases about my aunt's cake gone wrong.

"No!" I argue. "I know what I saw and felt. You just think I am crazy. I can't believe this."

"Serena!" she calls after me, but I storm away in the other direction toward my locker.

"We will talk about this tonight," she calls after me.

I let the late bell answer for me.

~

"WELL, I think that just about does it." Simon wipes the sweat from his brow with his forearm. "Thanks for your help, Serena."

"Since you're feeling so thankful, how about sharing the theme of my birthday booth with me?" I ask, nodding toward the red velvet curtained booth—a tradition that dates back as far back as I can remember.

Simon shakes his head. "Every year you try, and every year I say no. What makes this year any different?"

"I'm an adult now?" I offer.

"That means you can wait." He grins as he saunters off to my aunt's side.

"Girls, go get changed. We've got the rest of this," Aunt Odette calls out to my sisters and me. Aunt Odette looks wiped, with dark circles under her eyes. She always seems to be unwell around the carnival—fall allergies or something. Maybe it's the additional hours she invests to pull it off.

My sisters and I file into the house. When I return into the darkening night, I've traded paint-splattered overalls for a pair of jeans, a T-shirt, and my faux-leather jacket.

Nikki, Logan, and Max sit on the steps of my front porch, watching as the final rides are put together.

"Happy Birthday Part Two . . . and I am sorry. You're right, I should have listened." Nikki stands to hug me.

I stiffen at first and then ease into her, unable to remain mad at her for too long.

"You have to admit, it sounded crazy, but I am pretty sure I've approached you with crazier. I promise to keep an open mind. We will figure this out," she says.

"Thanks." I smile back, not feeling as alone and scared with her by my side.

"What was that all about?" Logan asks.

Nikki grins at me and says, "Serena wants to date me." And then she skips the two of us over to the unveiling of my booth.

Logan sighs as we both giggle. Worry still tugs at every corner of my mind, along with the need for answers, but it feels good to laugh and live in the moment.

Simon and Logan both pull aside the curtains on my "Paint Night" themed booth, complete with mini art kits for my friends as souvenirs.

We settle in to paint the Eiffel tower. I lose myself in the colors and textures until Logan elbows me.

"I know I'm not an artist, but since when was the Eiffel tower surrounded by waterfalls?"

I focus in on my painting, and my throat tightens.

Twin waterfalls box my tower in place.

Simon walks by, and I flag him down.

"Hey, where's Aunt Odette?" I ask.

"Oh, she's . . . around." He answers a little too quickly. "Why don't you hang out with your friends for now?"

He heads off to help someone before I can argue, and Nikki peers at my painting.

"Whoa, that's . . . something." She quiets, and I glance over at her. She checks her watch and then pastes a big smile on her face, leaping off her stool.

"Come on! Let's go explore before my shift at the kissing booth."

"Your what?" Max asks.

She pats his arm. "Anything for charity, baby."

"Come on, man," Logan says, clapping his shoulder. "Let's try to sneak into the Soothing Sips wine booth . . . That's your kinda thing, right?"

Max smiles, and they head off together, Logan's sudden effort distracting me.

"Well, that was unexpected," I joke. Nikki grins and hooks her arm through mine.

Weaving our way through the brightly lit cacophony of sounds and rides, we wave at people from school. The scents of fried dough and pumpkin spice lattes assault me, but the thought of food turns my stomach.

"Where are we going?" I ask.

"To get answers," she says.

Nikki pulls me to a dark purple velvet tent with a shimmering sign that proclaims, "Madame Tousseau."

"Oh, no," I mumble.

"What?" Nikki asks.

"You know I don't believe in this crap."

She glares at me.

"Okay, I'll rephrase that. *Your* terrible fortune telling is the only of its kind that I believe in."

"Hey!" She feigns hurt.

A middle-aged woman with fiery red hair and bright green eyes comes to the opening of the tent.

I blush, hoping she didn't hear my outburst, but from the way she smiles at me, I can tell she did.

I open my mouth to apologize, but the woman holds up a manicured hand.

"Eeeets quite alright," the woman says. "Zee soul needs to grow more. "Pleeeze, come seet." She gestures toward the flap of her tent.

"Oh, no. We were just looking," I say and turn to make my exit, nudging Nikki to keep moving.

Claws dig into my shoulder. I turn back and see the woman's sparkling red stiletto nails clinging to me, her face inches from mine. "You must be very careful, child. You are surrounded by eveeeel, and weeeell soon make a choice."

My heart thrums as Madame Tousseau fingers my necklace, dropping it immediately, as though it burns her, too.

"You are much more than you realize just yet." She pats my cheek. "Choose right, giyuuurl. Much eeeees at stake."

She disappears, leaving us outside of her tent, my heart pounding.

"Wow," Nikki whispers.

I stand, unmoving, staring at her tent.

"Are you okay?" she asks. "Freaking psychics. They leave you with more questions than answers."

"But, she went right for the necklace. Nik, that has to mean something," I say in a hushed tone.

"Serena," Nikki laughs. "She basically recited a fortune cookie.

37

You're a teenager, so 'young' with choices to make. The whole world is surrounded by evil, so that was ridiculously generic."

"But, she held the necklace like something is wrong with it," I protest.

"I'm sorry, but that is the ugliest rock I have ever laid eyes on. I feel like they zone in on noticeable accessories like that."

My lips twitch. *Maybe she's right.* When it's broken down like that, the whole thing sounds fake. Normally, I wouldn't have given it a second thought.

"Come on, let's geeeet you some vegan fried dough—if that's even a thing. Eeet's the least I can do, giyuuurl." Nikki mimics.

"I—" The necklace heats up against my skin, and I gasp. My heart slams into my ribcage.

"What now?" Nikki asks.

"I just need to go find Aunt Odette. I'll be back." I lose myself in the crowd, barely nodding at everyone who waves to me and dodging people who yell birthday wishes my way. I need to find her and finally confront her about this damn necklace.

I know that woman felt something, too.

I blow past the wine booth just in time to see Deputy Kasun stroll up behind Logan and Max as they change their master plan.

Logan calls out to me, but I don't stop, storming down each path. I pass the rides, just barely waving at Lena on the Ferris wheel.

Aunt Odette is nowhere to be found.

With a sigh of annoyance, I head to the waterside to plop down in defeat. That's when I hear a laugh that I had almost forgotten.

Mama?

I scramble to my feet and follow the sound, toward our backyard. There she is, treading water close to our little waterfall, in a white gown that matches the white gown Aunt Odette wears, beside her.

I hide behind my favorite weeping willow tree, peering out as men join them in the water. Mama flirts and laughs with . . . *Dr. Nance? From the hospital!* He set my arm when I broke it in second grade.

Dr. Nance swims out to her, along with the other men. The moonlight hits both her and my aunt in just the right way so that their skin shimmers—they look like goddesses afloat in the water.

Mama accepts Dr. Nance into her arms, lovingly stroking his cheek before planting her lips on his. Aunt Odette follows suit with one of the others.

"Mama?" I cry out, my voice carrying.

Why would she lie to us? All these years of guilt over her being sick and me living my life. Yet here she is, just fine. Doing awful things with these men who aren't my father.

I glance over to my right. A figure rustles the bushes. I narrow my eyes to get a better look at a man with something metallic glinting by his side. I lean in and connect eyes with his sea-glass green ones for a moment, and the breath freezes in my lungs.

Before I can focus in on more details, he backs away, slipping into a camouflage of greenery. Aunt Odette appears in front of me. Her dress clings to her soaked body.

"What the hell is going on?" I demand. "What happened to Mama? Who are those men, and what is wrong with you?"

Aunt Odette's eyes glow. She murmurs in a weird language, and my mind swirls into blackness.

CHAPTER 4

The final bell rings. I cringe. The headache I woke with after a late night at the Carnival still hits hard. Tylenol hasn't even taken the edge off. At least the weird brain fog has somewhat disappeared. I'd better not be getting sick. Homecoming is tomorrow.

Mr. Milner frowns. He's just getting revved up on his speech about what the founding fathers would think of the current administration. There's nothing he hates more than being interrupted. Groans from classmates turn into cheers since we have all been saved from it.

"Don't forget, your first project is due Monday. Extra points will be awarded to anyone who goes with a historical, non-fiction theme for their homecoming costume tomorrow. But, as you kids say nowadays, 'pictures, or it didn't happen'!" He chortles to himself as he fills his briefcase.

The groans return. Chairs scrape the floor, and we shuffle out the door into the neutral halls that only help to encourage the unshakeable wave of sleepiness that eighth period AP Government imparted.

I trip over a shin and bounce into the locker belonging to the sometimes pleasant, but mostly scary, Ellisyn Daryn. I wonder for probably the millionth time how the hell her mom, Stella, spawned Ellisyn, when Stella is such a calm, health-food-store-owning hippy.

Ellisyn's flint eyes bore through me, proving my point. She snaps,

"I know walking while talking must be such a challenge for you, but maybe try a little harder?"

"Uh, sorry," I squeak, hating myself for doing it.

"Don't you have a kitten to sacrifice or something?" Nikki shrills in my defense, appearing at my side.

Ellisyn's eyes narrow. "Watch it, Nikkola," she hisses. A dangerous smirk dances across her red lips. Strawberry-blond hair swings against the shoulders of her teal cashmere sweater.

Nikki's eyes flash.

Memories of the two girls joking in the halls mere months ago flash through my mind. Nikki always fit right into the fringe of the popular girls, even though she was just a teensy bit edgier than them.

I grab Nikki and pull her over to my own locker. "What happened between you two, again?" I ask, trying to fish for an answer that I was never given.

"What do you mean?" Nikki asks, playing with her hair.

"You guys were never best friends or anything, but you and Ellisyn were never this mean to each other. What happened?"

She shrugs. "I decided I was sick of hanging around that basic wi —basic bitch."

"Nik . . ."

"We don't have time for a friendtervention. I just grew up and realized there's more to life than matching my nail polish with my outfit and joining every school committee."

"Well, how about one committee or club?"

"I still belong to art club."

"It's just . . . I know there's stuff you aren't telling me, and it hurts."

She refuses to meet my eyes once more and says, "If something were wrong, you would be the first to know."

"Promise?" I ask.

She smiles, but it doesn't reach her eyes. "Promise," she repeats, hooking her pinky through mine.

"What's going on?" Logan asks, his face tightening into his serious look, taking in the tail end of our conversation. Max trails him like a confused, well-dressed puppy.

"Nothing, just girl stuff," I say.

"Speaking of which," Nikki says, "Bye, Felicias. We're going shopping."

"Oh." Logan looks a little disappointed and then glances at me. "Did you still want to meet at Burger Bar later?"

Oops! That one totally slipped my mind, along with a good chunk of whatever happened last night. I bite my lip, pondering. "Yeah, sure. After we are done," I say a little too quickly, distracted by trying to figure out why I feel like there's a hole in my memories.

Nikki pouts. "But we can't give you a set time, because there's no limit on how long it will take to find the perfect shoes."

Logan stares at her. "It's Callie's."

"And?"

"It's two floors. One shoe section. Not thinking it will take all night."

"Can we text you guys when we're done?" I ask.

Nikki sashays over to Max, whose skin-tight jeans and leather jacket are the polar opposite of Logan's daily uniform of flannel and denim.

Max is too busy digging in a black leather pouch at his hip to notice. He glances down from underneath a cocked fedora to briefly smile as Nikki presses her lips to his cheek.

"Sure, I guess," Logan says, his eyes widening in horror. "What. Is. That?" He points his finger at the pouch along Max's waist.

Max zips it shut, slinging the bag at an angle.

Nikki blinks. "It's a Gucci belt bag. They're all the rage in the city. Right, baby?" She tweaks Max's nose and nuzzles into his cheek, but Max merely clears his throat.

Logan's face turns red with the effort of stifling explosive laughter.

He doubles over, tears coming to his eyes when he manages to gasp out, "Fanny. Pack!" before completely losing it.

Nikki bristles. "No. It's a vintage Gucci belt bag, Mountain Man."

He doesn't even hear her and clanks back against my locker, shutting it, while he hoots with laughter.

"Um. I wasn't done in there yet," I grumble, but Nikki's words pique my attention.

I turn on my heel. "Max, do you understand how the skin is

actually removed from an animal to make something like that for you, which could just as easily be made from another material? Did you know that most of the animal is wasted after? So, you're basically walking around with a dead animal on your hip and back. Does that make you feel like a man?"

Logan guffaws. "Well, I think that ship has sailed. Because it's a *fanny pack*."

"Oh, for the love of God," Nikki says. "IT'S A BELT BAG FOR MEN."

Kids walking down the hall stop and stare, laughing as they pass us.

Nikki turns to Max, whose cheeks are just as red as Logan's.

She hugs him, cooing. "Don't listen to PETA and Joe Dirt over here. *You* are cutting edge. *They* are stuck in 2002."

"Max, if you're bored someday, come on over. I have a few documentaries that would fascinate you. Do you know how they make Uggs? It's extremely educational and eye-opening."

Logan bumps into me lightly. "I think he's suffering enough by having to wear that thing."

And then he cracks up again, shaking his head as he walks away from us.

Max glares down at Nikki, mumbling, "I told you it was a little much for . . . *here*."

"Hey, would you rather fit in with future L.L.Beaners of America?" She asks, fitting snuggly into his arm to walk him to his car.

"I'll meet you at the Jeep," she calls over her shoulder to me.

I turn back to my locker, thankful that I will be able to miss out on their little lovefest as I grab the rest of my books.

"Saving the world one leather good at a time, are we, Alverson?" Mr. Weaver, my art teacher, teases from behind.

I jump. He's good at sneaking up on people.

"Well, someone has to speak for the poor animals," I huff.

He holds his hands up. "Do your thang, girl. Speaking of which, when do you want to meet up to discuss your portfolio?"

On top of the dream, the necklace, Mama, Laurel, Lena, Nikki and Logan's weirdness, and really, the stress of creating something that reflects my abilities and goals after high school ends—I am beyond overwhelmed.

I snap. "Can I please just get through homecoming first?"

I slam my locker shut and whirl around to face my favorite teacher, waiting for him to go all "you will not talk to me like that, young lady" on me.

But, of course, he doesn't.

He just nods. "Cool, let it simmer. I can dig. Just don't let it burn to the bottom of the pan, 'kay?"

I nod.

"Have a good night, Alverson. Go reflect by a stream or something. You know, fresh air—nature."

He gestures past the open school entrance, where misty shades of indigo in the mountains mix with afternoon sun, dotted with aspen and pines. He's right. It's stunning and *should* be cathartic. Even though I am an artist, I sometimes take the beauty of my home for granted.

When I glance back, he's gone, sauntering down the hall, whistling a Grateful Dead riff.

I step out into the crisp fall air, squinting against the sun as I dig in my bag for my vintage Ray-Ban Wayfarers and slip them on.

Nikki's lithe body curves over the hood of my Jeep, leaning against it. Her forehead's full of lines as she furiously taps away at her phone.

"You know what I won't miss about this place?" she asks.

I pause at the driver's side door. "Uh . . . flannel, lack of malls, hiking boots?"

"Well, yeah. You would think they could make some fashionable hiking accessories. I mean, they have cute skiing stuff."

"Well, if your indie music label doesn't pan out, there you go," I say.

She rolls her eyes. "The mountain reception is what I won't miss. I've been trying to text Max for like five minutes now, and it won't send."

We both get into the Jeep and buckle up before I place the key in the ignition. I glance over at her, my shoulders sagging. "You're kidding, right?"

"What?"

"You just left him. Max is awesome, but—girl time. Remember? We're gonna see him in a couple hours, anyway."

She slides down in her seat. Letting out a sigh, she drawls. "You're right, I'm sorry. He just . . . smells so good, and he's so cute, and his hair is so soft and curls in my hand. Did I say that it's soft?"

"Where the hell did my best friend go?"

"To Seattle, with Max, in her mind," Nikki says.

My gaze remains fixed on her, and I leave my eyebrows pointing toward the sky. "Girl, I love you. And it's because I love you that I am going to cling to the string of your balloon. Remember Aaron?"

She scrunches her nose. "Blah, forest ranger mistake."

"And Bill?"

"That was my jock phase," she says flippantly.

"Cameron?"

"The name alone says it all." She sticks her tongue out in an *I'm gonna puke* face.

"Yeah, but you were gonna 'go to Seattle' with all of them." I air quote with my fingers, looking over my shoulder to make sure that all is clear before backing out. I point the Jeep toward town square and Callie's.

"You're jealous," she snaps, incredulous.

Stopping at the stop sign on the corner of Main and First, I let a couple of kids cross.

I scoff. "Jealous of what? Losing myself in a high school thing and turning into a pod person? No thanks."

I chance a look over at her crestfallen face, and my throat tightens. "Aw, Nik, I'm sorry. I didn't mean it. I'm stressed between school, worrying about *you*, worrying about Lena, and this weird necklace thing. I swear Aunt Odette is hiding something."

She rubs my shoulder, proving why she's my bestie for life. Even after a low blow like that, she is still right there for me, for whatever reason.

"Deep breath. Okay? First off, please don't worry about me. For the bajillionth time, I'm cool."

But even the way she says it indicates otherwise.

"We will just be there for Lena, and kick whoever's ass we need to. It's all we can do. As far as the necklace and your aunt, we will figure that out, too. Okay?"

I take a deep breath and nod, lucky to find an open spot on the street in front of Callie's Consignments. I pull in, beating a red Honda Civic. Nikki sticks her tongue out at the driver in victory.

Usually this street is so packed that the two-hour parking allotment is strictly overseen by a guy named Travis. No one seems to know much about him other than he is rumored to have flunked out of police school. Everyone thinks that's why he takes his job way too seriously. He lurks in alleys, waiting to strike if you are thirty seconds late to your car.

"Oh, shoot!" I cry out, remembering that I am wearing my reclaimed Ramones shirt. I frantically dig around in the back seat until I unearth one of Laurel's cardigans.

"What?" Nikki asks as she watches me slip into the very un-me sweater. "Oh, honey. We need to talk about your current life choices . . ."

"No! This shirt . . . Remember? Callie explicitly threated my life over Frankensteining it, and I sort of swore that I wouldn't. I mean, my fingers were crossed behind my back, but . . ."

"Joey Ramone would totally be down with your improvements," she muses. "But I can see both sides."

"Thanks for the diplomacy," I mutter as I slide out of the Jeep and grab my bag.

Nikki's phone beeps, and she pumps her fist in the air.

Imitating the SpongeBob announcer, she says, "Fifteen meeenutes laaaaterrrr, my text went through."

She furiously taps away at her phone, glancing up in apology. "Two more minutes, and then I'm yours." Nikki finishes her text and slips her phone into her bag.

I open the door to Callie's, chimes tinkling. The familiar smell is one part countless stories that each article of clothing holds, and two parts musky floral incense. I would recognize the scent anywhere.

"Time to do some damage! Hey, Callie," Nikki chirps to the

gorgeous brunette bent over the register, helping a customer decide between two shirts.

"Did you get any new shoes for homecoming?" Nikki asks.

Callie straightens up so she stands tall. Her long, wavy hair brushes her shoulders as she points us toward the far end of the store. The newly-curated homecoming display beckons.

Callie's sparkling bluish-green eyes, a sharp contrast to her dark hair, shrink to slits, letting us know that she's watching.

"We mean the shoes no harm. Plus, Serena is on her best behavior because she loves her Fendi." Nikki winks at her, pointing toward my purse. I try to sneak by, but Callie has hawk eyes. She focuses in on my shirt. I wrap the sweater tightly around myself and then slip between racks of dresses.

"So, what shoes would a serial killer's mother wear to homecoming? Sensible or sexy?" Nikki muses. "I need to get in character."

"We aren't actresses."

"Speak for yourself, girly. There are no small roles in life."

"It's a dance."

"It's the last homecoming of our high school career—and more importantly, senior prank kickoff. Get your head in the game, Alverson. Did you find a good pair of scream queen shoes, yet?"

"Not quite."

"Don't worry, we will find something. Worst case, your dress will cover whatever you wear. This detail will not trip up our diabolical scheme."

"Diabolical scheme" is our play on the homecoming theme of love-struck characters from history and movies.

Logan, Max, and I decided it would just be easier to give into Nikki's whims for one of the last times. In her defense, it's sort of a hilarious plot. The only part that's making me feel a little weird is that she is pairing Logan and I off as Carrie White and Tommy Ross, partners in crime to her Mrs. Voorhees and Max's Jason. Because holding a dance for teens on Friday the 13th is an amazing idea, said no adult, ever.

Nikki holds up a pair of white kitten heels and shrugs.

"Perfect!" I say, because I hate high heels, like the pair Nikki tucks under her arm, even more than I hate algebra.

We head toward the register, passing a pile of garments that Callie is in the process of adding to the racks on the floor. Nikki grabs a light blue vintage Jackie O–style hat.

"This is perfect for our cover story," she says, referring to the fake costumes the four of us are planning to wear for parent pictures, before changing into our prank costumes later at school.

"Tab, please, for mine," I mouth as Callie answers the ringing phone.

While she wraps it all up and rings Nikki out, I thank her for her help with my new purse. Then I venture to the back of her store, taking inventory of my handmade jewelry. I count each of the glass-bead, wire-coiled bracelets, rings, necklaces, and earrings, tracking what needs to be replenished. This is what keeps my clothing tab running strong.

On my way out the door, I wave to Callie, and she offers me a tiny side-smile. Out of everyone who lives in Havenwood Falls, Callie and I possibly have the strangest relationship.

"Burger Bar now?" Nikki asks, fishing for her phone. "I'll text the guys. They will be happy that we finished early."

I glance at my watch, my shoulders relaxing when I realize we haven't been parked in front of Callie's for the full two hours yet. Aunt Odette has threatened my Jeep privileges if I bring home another parking ticket. We aren't supposed to meet the guys for half an hour. I told Logan we would be there by six o'clock. It's closing in on five-thirty, but it's never a bad thing to get there a little early, because it's always packed, no matter the day of the week.

We settle into the Jeep after dumping our bags in the backseat. I back out into traffic and head back toward school, pulling into the Burger Bar parking lot across the street from Havenwood Falls High.

The Burger Bar lot is basically a mirror image of the school lot after classes end, just add women on roller skates and trays of burgers and fries hooked onto the car doors.

"You know, I think this is all that we have here that actually impresses Max. He said that drive-in burger places are hard to find on the outside," Nikki muses.

"Oh, that's not all that impresses him here." I wink at her as I pull into an empty spot, and she blushes.

"We're going in, right?" I ask hopefully, not really wanting my Jeep to reek of burgers.

"We can eat inside if you want." Nikki smiles, knowing me too well.

We step out of the Jeep and weave our way through the crowd. I wave to our friend, Paisley Underwood, but she doesn't look up from her new boyfriend, Cole Silver, and I sigh.

"You shouldn't worry about me," Nikki says. "*She* is the one we both need to worry about."

Paisley has started skipping school and her shifts at Coffee Haven, where she works, since she started dating Cole.

The door swings open and "Love Me Do" by the Beatles croons from the jukebox in the corner. Logan and Max wave to us from the counter, where they're saving us a couple of stools. Ha, and here I thought we were the early ones.

"Hey, kids!" Maggie, co-owner of Burger Bar, waves. She pivots on her skates to deposit ketchup at a table occupied by Kase, Greg, Joe, the other football guys, and some cheerleaders, her chestnut curls flying behind her.

"Hey, Mags! Any new menu items?" I ask.

Maggie pulls a pad of paper and a pen from the pocket of her apron. "Yeah, good luck with your save-the-whales-tofurger-pitch today. Frank's in a mood."

"HELEN!" he barks from behind the grill, as if proving his wife's point.

Helen Rigby, a brunette I have only seen in passing at town events, bumps into the counters and stools, making her way over to the window to see what he wants.

"What did I say about abbreviations? Is this an order of rings or wings? It can't be both, sweetheart . . ."

Her face crumples. Maggie waves to us apologetically and then skates over to help, not even bothering to leave us menus, because we all but live here.

We settle into counter seats, casually observing as Helen rips her apron off and then half skates, half soldier-crawls out the front door.

Frank slams the spatula on the grill. "I'm deducting the cost of any uniform items or skates that aren't returned from your final paycheck!" He yells after Helen, but she is already gone.

"He's gonna give himself a heart attack," Logan says, shifting on his stool so that his knee touches mine.

I slowly move my leg away. "One more reason to serve healthier food here. Maybe he will start eating it."

Nikki groans. "We're all gonna die. Let Frank live his best life, will you, Serena?"

Maggie skates back over and takes our orders, and then Frank comes out with a tray full of plates for the football players' table.

I glance over at them, and Ben Siddons, one of Logan's teammates, makes kissy faces at me until he sees Logan's and Frank's matching glares.

Frank and Maggie were school friends of Mama's and friendly with Daddy when he first came to Havenwood Falls. Even though Frank is gruff when it comes to my dietary choices, he and Maggie have always looked out for my sisters and me when it comes to stuff like this, since neither of my parents are here to do it.

When Frank stops at the counter with our food and places a wilted plate of lettuce and tomatoes in front of me, I wrinkle my nose. "Oh, come on."

"What?" Frank barks.

"What is this?" I ask.

"A salad."

"No, it's old lettuce and a mushy tomato."

He points to the flashing neon sign that screams "Burger Bar."

"Can you read? Does that say 'salad bar?' No. It's Burger Bar. If you want falafel, head to Denver."

"Did you ever stop to think that it would be better karma for you to serve more plant-based choices? Cheaper, too, *and* you could make more money. It's a win-win."

"You know, Frank, some of that stuff is actually good." Logan takes a sip from his soda. *What is he doing?*

The vein in Frank's neck bulges. "Serena's hippy not-meat will never touch my grill!"

"Come on, man. Don't you want to give Stella a run for her money? You do know she started selling baked goods at Health Nut, right?" Logan asks.

Frank scowls.

"What if she steals your pie business?" Max pipes up, after swallowing a big bite of his burger.

"When you're the little guy, you've gotta keep up, or you'll be lost in the dust of your competition," Max says. "I used to see businesses fold like that all the time in the city."

Frank snorts. "Well, this isn't the city, and I am NOT the little guy, Tight Pants. Stella isn't even running a diner. I am."

Logan cringes over-dramatically. "Yeah, man . . . I don't know. I saw some tables and chairs being delivered to her last week. She's really pushing the whole café vibe with her smoothies and healthy takeout."

Frank continues to frown, but I can tell that he's thinking about it.

I grin at Logan, and then he bumps against my knee again, and I stop smiling. I clear my throat, turning my attention back to Frank.

"People are waking up to the reality that agricultural monopolies are in bed with the government. Stella is realizing a new consumer need and capitalizing on it." I say.

"You know what the problem is with your delusional generation?" Frank asks.

"No, but I'm sure you're going to tell us," Nikki answers before taking a sip of her chocolate milkshake.

"Your problem is that you kids are so busy with your 'Netflix and relax' that you've forgotten how to work and think for yourselves."

"Chill," Max says.

Frank's nostrils flare, and he starts to walk over to Max, who looks like he's ready to bolt.

"No, Frank! Max means the saying is 'Netflix and chill.'" Logan rushes to Max's defense. Max stares, wide-eyed, and Nikki smiles at

Logan, flashing every tooth in her head. Logan shakes his head and looks away.

I sigh and then stand and walk over to Frank, gently placing a hand on his arm. "Don't you want to come in at the ground level of that cash cow, like Stella?" If nothing else speaks to him, perhaps money will entice him.

"Sure, as long as I can chop that cow up and throw her on my grill," Frank fires back.

I gasp, and Maggie skates up in between us. "Ya know, I don't make enough for this. Frank, in the kitchen. Serena, hon, I can whip up a new salad for you."

Frank says, "We are out of lettuce."

Logan glares at him, then turns to me. "How about we walk over to Health Nut and grab you something?"

"It's fine. Forget it," I say as I sink back onto my stool and try to spear a slimy tomato with my fork.

"It's on the house." Maggie winks at me, and then heads into the kitchen after her husband.

"Since when are you into veganism, Mr. Football Star?" Nikki teases.

Logan turns red. "Shut up, Nik."

"Since you've decided to be into a vegan?" Nikki continues, leaning behind me at an unnatural angle so she can flick his ear.

Logan's football team hoots and hollers, waving him over. *Thank God for the interruption.* They yell something about meeting them down at the river. Part of me hopes Logan will join them, because the elephant between us is taking up way too much room. Logan smiles at them but declines, tossing a fry at Nikki's head to silence her.

It's about seven o'clock when we finally surrender our little corner of the Burger Bar counter and step out into the chilly evening.

"Do you want a ride home, guys?" I ask Nikki and Max, but I've already lost them to Lover's Lane.

Nikki hugs me. "I think we're gonna take a little walk. Can I grab my shoes tomorrow?"

It's officially serious. She's ditching designer for dude.

"Sure, no problem. See ya guys." I hug her back.

They wave and then take off, cutting through the square to go sit in the gazebo, where the twinkle lights glimmer against the setting sun.

"You and Max seemed to get along okay tonight." I say to Logan, once Max and Nikki are safely out of earshot.

"I guess it wasn't horrible. So, what are you up to? Coffee?" he asks with that weird gleam in his eye again.

"Aw, sorry. I can't. I have a stop to make, and then homework."

His eyes are on me, and I can't bring myself to look back at him, because I know I will get sucked in to saying yes, when I have other things on my mind that need to be handled.

"Karina," he says, more than asks.

My throat tightens. "How do you do that?"

"Do what?"

"Know everything. Even the things I don't really want to say."

He smirks. "Because I know you better than *you* know you. Well, enough to know that I need to quit while I'm ahead, because you want to be alone with her. Have a good night, Rena."

His chin grazes the top of my head when he wraps his arms around me. I give him an awkward half-hug in return, then he waves and heads toward his truck.

I stand at the door of the Jeep, watching him leave, and it hits me.

He's right. He knows me entirely too well. Maybe that's the problem.

THE SUN PAINTS the sky shades of orange, coral, and yellow as I pull into the cemetery parking lot.

I step along the stone walkway, lined with flowers and foliage, walking past the tombstones and walls lined with plaques. This is the main cemetery, but since my family is a founding family, our burial grounds are in a different area.

In the darkest corner of the graveyard, behind the moss and ivy that line the stone wall, I reach for a handle. The door creaks open to reveal a dank stone tunnel that smells of mildew. A steady dripping echoes in the distance. As much as I hope it is just my imagination, I swear something scurries by my feet.

I activate the flashlight feature of my cell phone and quicken my pace. Whenever I walk this tunnel, I always picture the "other mother" scenes from *Coraline*. I don't care how old I am, it always makes me want to run to the tunnel's exit.

A similar door to the one I just opened appears in front of me. I open it and let myself back out into the chilly evening. A slight breeze rustles the aspen leaves, feathering them against the sherbet sky. I grab Laurel's sweater, which still lays in my bag, and slip it on, wrapping myself in the thin yarn. I step through the elaborate marble arch of the cemetery reserved for the Old Families.

Cooley Creek babbles in the distance. A few stray birds chirp, here and there, as they make their way home for the night. I crunch over twigs and fallen leaves. The familiar chill rushes through me when I cross in front of the weeping angel statue. She is mossy with the years she has spent perched up there, judging the souls of all who enter her realm.

With a shudder, I break eye contact with the creepy thing and make my way through the unkempt pathway that nature has reclaimed. I step deeper into the cemetery, over a hill, into a more secluded, older portion of the land, where caged graves sporadically break up the horizon line of tombstones.

The first grave at the top of a small hill hollows my heart, as usual.

I trail my fingers over the lone, weathered stone with a crack in it and whisper, "Hey, Henry."

Not that I knew him. I mean, he died in 1902, but the fact that he died at 16, his tombstone a riddle of one name that could've been either his first or last, and the way his plot is isolated . . . it makes me sad. Nobody should be alone in death. I have sort of adopted him and can't set foot in the cemetery without checking in.

The breeze picks up again, whipping my hair in my face. The tinkle of hundreds of colorful glass ball chimes, strung up in the trees, trill. They float in the air, bumper-carring against each other, but somehow not breaking. This is the entrance to my family's plot. Regardless of my grand plans to see the world, I can feel it deep down

—one day, this is where I will lie. My bones will return to the same corner of earth where they were born. As much as that thought bothers me, as much as I plot to run from this place once I can, it oddly brings a sense of comfort to know where I will end up.

I pass random stones belonging to older ancestors I have heard mentioned once or twice in passing, tapping the stone of the true patriarch of our family, Jedidiah Alverson.

Three smaller tombstones surround his—the resting places of his daughters: Maude, Esther, and Josie. I pause to examine Josie's headstone, and the crystal of my necklace finds its way into my hand, of its own volition. I had never really paid her grave much attention before, but now that I wear a piece of jewelry that was clearly important to her, I feel as though I should.

I drop the crystal back onto my chest, run my fingers over the cold limestone of Josie's grave marker, and then turn away to the grave I truly came for.

Karina's creamy marble tombstone is not nearly as old as all the rest. I pull out the roundie blanket I have wrapped up in my purse, unfurling it over her grave. I lay down on my side and dig out my sketchpad, a smaller tin of Prismacolor pencils, and a box of drawing charcoal.

Settling into silence, I pick up the dying glint of sunshine on the glass ball chimes in the trees, trying to capture the exact gleam and the gem tone hues on my gray paper, before finally speaking up.

"So, there's something weird about this necklace of yours, Karina," I say.

For whatever reason, it's just easier for me to talk to her like that. Really, at death, she was younger than I am right now, so it just feels weird to call her "aunt."

The tinkling glass in the trees is the only response I am given. I treat it as though she nods her white-blond head, sending me an encouraging smile, so I continue.

"I feel like I am going crazy even saying this, but it burns me. The first night I put it on, as soon as I set foot in water, it all but blew up into a crazy light show. Mama freaked out when she saw me wearing it, too. It was the first time she has responded in so long . . .

it has to mean something. But Aunt Odette blew it off like it was nothing."

I trail off and swap out a magenta pencil for white so I can work in some more streaks of light. I reach for the twisted cardboard stump from my charcoal pencil tin so that I can blend it, all the while imagining how this aunt I have never met would respond.

"There's more." I breathe out. "Something is wrong with me—with my body." Content, for now, with the scarlet glass ball, I swap the white pencil out for dahlia purple and start working on its neighbor.

"I still haven't gotten . . . you know." I sigh. "It's so stupid that it's hard for me to say. It's not like I'm in middle school and this is all new. It's not like anyone is here. *You* aren't even technically here." My voice shrinks, and tears dot my lashes.

"I'm sorry. I didn't mean it like that. Of course, you're here. I just wish you were on this side of the soil. I feel like you would be different. Mama—she isn't well enough for me to dump my problems on. She needs me to be strong for her. So does Aunt Odette. Plus, whenever I try to talk to her, she changes the subject."

I put my pencils down and hold my sketchpad out to critique my work. Then I place the pad down and crack my knuckles before stretching.

"All the medical tests came out okay . . . but I feel like she's hiding something from me. We have been fighting about college, too. She knows how badly I want to go away, but the guilt over leaving her, the girls, and Mama keeps me here. I feel like sometimes she uses it to manipulate me. Why doesn't she want me to leave?"

I ball up, my arms around my knees, as I lean in to her grave marker. Cool marble calms my fiery cheeks. I blubber all over my dead aunt's grave, wishing she could actually give me advice.

A rustling in the distance bolts me upright. Eyeliner smears the back of my hand as I try to destroy the evidence of my tears.

"Hello?" I rasp.

Nothing.

Anger flames in my belly, and I yell, "Hey! Creeper! Get your freak on somewhere else!"

There's more rustling, and this time a dark form emerges from the shadows. His sea-glass green eyes lock onto mine, and I forget how to breathe. A hazy memory of a man with the same eyes, with a knife, standing by the waterside, smacks into me. I take off running toward the tunnel.

My heart pounds as footsteps follow.

CHAPTER 5

*W*hen I get to the Jeep, I fumble with the key, hands shaking. I look over my shoulder and all around me. No one. But I don't allow myself to be lulled into a false sense of security as I finally get into the Jeep and lock the doors, taking off down Main Street.

It's only then that I realize I must have kept my notebook and my new purse in my hands all along, because luckily, they are on the seat next to me, unlike my blanket. *Damn, I really loved that one—but there's no way I am going back for it.*

I somehow make it home in one piece, which is a small miracle. The entire ride was spent debating whether or not to go to the sheriff's office and report the strange guy in the woods. And what was up with that weird image of a similar figure by the water on my property with a knife? It was like déjà vu, but I have never seen anyone so creepy before.

"Ow!" A deep voice cries out.

I jump, so lost in my own thoughts that I hadn't realized that I walked into the tavern, instead of the cabin as I intended, smacking the door into someone. I peer around the door and come face to face with a slightly annoyed Simon.

"Oh, sorry. Didn't see you."

His forehead crinkles as he looks at me. "Hey, what's wrong? You're shaking."

I plop down onto a leather armchair next to the roaring fire, my adrenaline rush finally wearing out.

"What were you doing outside in just a sweater?" He asks, standing to his full height. His biceps and chest muscles flex under a white T-shirt that he somehow manages to keep clean, even after hours spent over a hot stove and grill.

Simon runs one of his large hands through his trimly cut, loose light brown curls, his bright blue eyes flashing in concern. "Serena?"

"I was in the cemetery, talking to Karina, and this creepy guy was there. He chased me."

Simon stands straighter. "Did he hurt you? Why were you alone in the woods at night like that? Why didn't you take Logan or Nikki with you?"

I flinch, still confused, feeling like I am stuck between the waking world and a dream.

"I'm calling Sheriff Kasun," he says, reaching for his cell phone.

"No, just . . . maybe it wasn't anything."

"We need to discuss this with your aunt when she gets home. She took the girls to town. I still think that the police need to know someone is lurking in the woods like that."

"Maybe it was just a guy from school. I don't know. I am so tired, and I was already upset, talking to Karina, maybe it was my imagination."

The concern in his face deepens, so I move to change the subject before he pokes around any further. If my aunt is the Narnian White Witch, Simon is the damn trees, or that little dwarf with the whip.

"What were you doing back there, anyway?" I ask, nodding toward the door.

He rolls his eyes and saunters over to the bar, pouring himself a beer and popping on the switch for the hot water kettle. "Patching a wall. Let's just say it was an eventful evening here at the Fallview."

"Really? On a school night?" I joke weakly, desperate to move on.

"Two words," he says. "Drunk Rocas."

"Huh, please continue."

"Tase thought that Xandru was hitting on Addie, only—*plot twist* —he was actually here alone, and she was at home. Besides, everyone knows Xan is back with Kaela. Smart choice on Maddie's part to stay home. Tase drank so much that he thought she was with him, so he and Xan wound up tossing fists, and then chairs, until Tase almost fell off the patio into the damn falls. I managed to save him, but then he thought *I* was trying to hit on Maddie, so he swung at me. I ducked, and he nailed Xan *again*. I finally got hold of both those numbskulls and tried to throw them out, and then Xan kicked a hole in the wall." He mutters something else before taking a swig of his beer.

"I was trying to patch it up for now, until I can actually take care of it properly, so Odette doesn't freak out." He eases down into the leather armchair across from me after handing me my steaming cup of green tea.

I smile my thanks to him. "Bet you never expected this sleepy little town to be so exciting when you came here."

He laughs. "Oh, I had an idea. It's always the quiet ones that tend to have the best story behind them—that goes for people as well as places. Speaking of story, how's the art thing going?"

I cock an eyebrow. "My 'art thing'? That's the technical term you're using, huh?"

He grins. "Hey, we aren't all as cultured as you are—going places." Something in the way he says that saddens me.

"Simon, don't talk like that. You run this entire place most of the time, because Aunt Odette is so busy with Mama. Stop picking on yourself."

The grin returns to his face. "Aw, you care?" He jokes.

"Hell yeah, I care. Because if anyone is going to make fun of you, it'd better be me."

He whips the pillow from his chair at my head, narrowly missing my steaming mug.

Simon goes on about something in the background, but a vision of Aunt Odette and Mama, floating in the water, wearing matching white gowns washes over me. It's the same déjà vu sensation that I had in the cemetery before I was chased.

My heart races, and my chest burns where the necklace rests

against it. Simon calls my name in the background, but I am too distracted by the skin on my chest all but sizzling.

I yelp and jump from my chair. Burning tea spills all over my lap. The ceramic mug clatters to the floor, where it's reduced to shards.

Simon jumps to his feet, handing me a towel from a nearby table. "Are you okay?"

I blink, shake my head, and accept the towel, patting my lap dry. It doesn't make any sense! Mama won't even take a bath without prescribed tranquilizers, let alone walk downstairs to get to the waterfall.

"I'm going to call your aunt." Simon grabs his phone again.

"No. Please. I'm fine. It's been a weird night." *More like week . . .*

Simon narrows his eyes, assessing me.

"Please don't call her. I just want my pencils, paper, some tea, and quiet."

I bend down to clean up my mess.

Simon waves me off. "Why don't you let me take care of that? I can make you another cup of tea to go. Styrofoam is Serena-proof."

"Not Styrofoam. It never breaks down." I sigh.

He smiles. "That was a test. I wasn't going to let you out of here if you let that one fly."

I laugh weakly as he replaces my tea in one of the biodegradable cups I convinced Aunt Odette to order.

I take the cup and then reach up to give him a hug. "Thanks, Simon. For, you know. Listening to me."

My voice comes out tiny and tired. I wish I could tell him more. I know he is cool, but no grown-up is that cool, no matter how many video games they own.

"Hey, do me a favor and get to bed. Okay? Tomorrow's a big day," he says, reminding me about homecoming.

"And an even bigger day for you," I tease.

Due to her fallout with Aurelia and some other drama at school, Lena has decided not to come to the dance after all, even with my friends and me. To soften the blow, Simon offered to take her to do whatever she wants. Lena chose an indie movie festival in Grand Junction, the closest largish town, which is a two-hour drive away.

Simon groans. "Please don't remind me. She just looked so sad. I wanted to fix it, and before I knew it, I was agreeing to subtitles. You should never have to read a movie."

"Don't forget, jeans do not count as dress clothes," I say.

"God, I have to dress up, too? What fresh hell is this? How about jeans without holes?"

I snort.

He walks me to the door. "I mean it. Bed."

I nod and head out into the chilly night, wishing it was warmer so I could draw outside. I follow the path to the house, trying to ignore the way the rushing water tugs at me.

Once in my room, I change into flannel jammies. I settle in at my desk, by the window, drawing the falls until I can no longer keep my eyes open.

CHAPTER 6

"*W*here's Laurel?" Aunt Odette asks, searching the first floor of the house while Logan, Max, and I sit in the living room with Nikki and her parents, waiting to leave for homecoming.

"She went upstairs," Aunt Brynna says.

"Laurel?" Aunt Odette calls up the stairs.

"Can you please help me? My hair keeps falling out of the clips," Laurel whines from the bathroom, her voice panicked.

"Must be serious if she said please," Logan mutters.

Nikki snorts.

A few minutes later, Aunt Odette and Laurel emerge. Laurel's lacy, one-shoulder peach dress sets off her creamy skin. Her hair pinned into a curly up-do reveals the same delicate neck and shoulders all the Alverson women share. My breath falters. *Where did my baby sister go?*

"Laurel, you look amazing!" I say.

Her cheeks flush as she takes a seat next to the fireplace.

"So where is this guy?" Uncle Christian asks, not sounding too thrilled.

"Turner should be here soon." Laurel's grin sparkles like sunshine dancing on water. I find myself mirroring her because it's one of the first times she has been this happy in a while. Hard as I am on her, and as frustrating as she can be, she's still my sister, and it's good to see her like this.

"Well, before he gets here and I 'embarrass Laurel,' let's talk, kids." Aunt Odette dangles the Jeep keys midair.

Her voice takes on a dangerous turn, and she eyes me, as though I don't drive her Jeep every day. "You drink and drive, and it won't be Sheriff Kasun you'll have to fear. Understood?"

"Don't worry, Aunt O. I refuse to be the dead chick who peaked in high school. I have people and industries to conquer," Nikki says, shooting a pointed stare at Aunt Brynna, who narrows her eyes in response.

What is going on with them?

"Although . . ." Nikki's face softens. "If it's *Deputy* Kasun coming at me with cuffs, let's just say I won't exactly resist arrest. Sorry, not sorry, Max." She winks at her boyfriend, as if it will make up for drooling over one of Sheriff Kasun's hot sons.

Uncle Christian turns an impressive shade of purple.

Aunt Odette eyes us before raising her hands in surrender. "Okay, okay. Just doing the obligatory parenting PSA thing. I really do trust you girls, but that's an easy thing to ruin."

She kisses us both on the cheek and then points two fingers toward her eyes and then to Logan's and Max's.

"I'm watching you, boys." Aunt Odette's voice chills the air.

Max visibly gulps.

Logan huffs. "Oh, for crying out loud, Odette. You know I would run in front of a car for all three of them. Obviously, I won't let Fanny Pack over here touch them, but, I mean, he wears a fanny pack, so I think we're all safe."

"IT'S. A. BELT. BAG." Max and Nikki protest simultaneously.

Nikki takes it one step further and grins at Aunt Odette. "You changed Logan's diapers once or twice, right? Zero threat."

A big smile and a tiny squeak emanate from Nikki as Logan chases her. Max stands there, looking like he might puke.

"Nikkola!" Aunt Brynna chides, rushing after her.

Uncle Christian rolls his green eyes and mouths, *"I'm so sorry."*

A cell phone rings in the background. Laurel digs her phone from her purse and disappears into the kitchen.

Aunt Brynna steps between Nikki and Logan, swatting at Nikki's hair, trying to fix it and separate her and Logan, whom she fixes with a set stare.

Logan clears his throat, adjusts his suit jacket, and then returns to my side on the couch. I pet his arm and smirk as he grumbles to himself.

"Okay, get out before you blow the house down," Aunt Odette jokes.

She commands us to line up in the backyard, with the waterfall in the background of the pictures. Aunt Brynna and Uncle Christian jump in, encouraging it, so we grudgingly give into the parents.

"If even one drop of water gets on my dress . . ." Nikki whines as we line up, backs facing the falls.

"It's water." Uncle Christian deadpans.

"It's *vintage*." Nikki huffs.

Laurel finally returns, her eyes red-rimmed.

"Hey, what's wrong?" I ask.

"Turner is meeting me at the dance," she says quietly.

"What about pictures?" Aunt Brynna asks. Aunt Odette touches her arm gently to silence her.

Nikki holds her hand out. "Give me your phone. I'll have that floaty turd here in five minutes or less."

"God, NO!" Laurel says, stuffing her phone in her purse and coming to my side.

I wrap my arm around her shoulder and kiss her cheek.

"I'm sorry," I whisper into her ear, knowing she doesn't want a scene.

"Come on, I'm very persuasive." Nikki waggles her eyebrows at Laurel.

Laurel shakes her head. "It's fine, pictures are lame. Just like the dumb dance theme."

She and Turner apparently have opted out of costumes.

I squeeze her again, and she leans in to me for a minute before wriggling free.

"Speaking of costumes," Uncle Christian says to Nikki. "Who are you and Max actually supposed to be? I know Serena and Logan are those two doofuses from Titanic."

"Hey! That's the movie we met during!" Aunt Brynna says.

"Please save us the high-school-English-field-trip-love-at-first-sight story." Nikki begs.

Uncle Christian smiles.

"Actually, Serena and Logan are Romeo and Juliet." Aunt Odette corrects.

"We're Jas—" Max begins.

Nikki's eyes fly open. She tackles her boyfriend into a kiss to shut him up. Max's arms fly out at his sides in surprise.

Uncle Christian is between them within seconds, Max trying to extricate himself, as Nikki grins up at her father.

"Hi, Daddy!" Nikki says.

He eyes her.

"We're Jackie O. and JFK." Nikki points to the tiny vintage hat we found at Callie's yesterday that perfectly matches her baby blue A-line dress. She slips on an oversized pair of black shades.

"Well, now that you have the glasses, it's obvious." Uncle Christian shakes his head at his daughter.

Aunt Odette sighs. "I wish that Lena and Simon were here for this. It just feels off without them."

They left earlier this morning so they would make it to Grand Junction on time for the movie festival.

"Wait, I almost forgot!" Logan jogs over to his truck. When he comes back he has a tiny plastic box in his hands.

My eyes question him, and Nikki and Aunt Odette say "awwww" in the background as he unwraps a delicate corsage. A white Calla lily, my favorite flower, surrounded by red roses.

"Oh, Logan . . . it's beautiful! You didn't have to."

"A little bird told me not to show up without it." He glances at Nikki, who winks.

Logan's eyes don't meet mine as he slides it onto my wrist.

I reach into the box and take out the matching boutonniere.

Logan winces. "I have to?"

I shrug. "Guess so."

He takes a breath and moves closer.

I glance over at Aunt Odette for assistance, because I've never done this before. She skirts over to my side, showing me how to pin it to his jacket.

"Thanks for not stabbing me," Logan teases.

"That comes later," Max cracks under his breath.

Nikki snickers.

I smooth the flowing tulle of my white gown and run my fingers through my blond hair. Aunt Odette braided the sides, forming a crown. She left the rest down, in curls that tumble past my shoulders.

Logan follows my lead, awkwardly smoothing the front of his vintage 1970s polyester suit, looking as uncomfortable as ever. He refused to even set foot in Callie's, so we were lucky to find his suit on eBay.

"The things I do for you," he says softly.

I grin up at him and ruffle his hair. He catches my hand in his on its way down, not relinquishing it as the flashes explode around us.

A cool breeze picks up, goosebumps dot my arms and chest, and hair tickles my face. I move the strands stuck to my glossy lips. A few drops of water stray from the waterfall. Carried on the wind, they land on my shoulder blade. The necklace burns me so intensely that I cry out and jump.

"Hey!" Logan says in alarm, hands hovering over me, ready to take out any imaginary threat.

I take a deep breath, and the burning sensation is gone. It's one of those things that happens so fast and so randomly that you question its actual existence.

"Serena?" Aunt Odette asks.

Oh, you know. This psychotic necklace that you gave me keeps burning me. Or, even better, I am losing my mind. File that under conversations not to have in front of most of the people you know before heading to a dance.

"Uh . . . rock in my shoe," I lie.

Aunt Brynna openly glares at me.

I gulp, blinking, and then she's looking just as concerned as the rest. *Am I seriously going insane?*

"You good?" Logan asks softly.

"Yeah."

He bumps my shoulder conspiratorially. "You know, I'm cool with sitting this out. A man's pants should never be this tight."

"Are you sure, Serena?" Aunt Odette asks, not taking her eyes off me. Everything in me begs to tell her the truth. I promise myself that tonight will be the night that I tell her everything and get some answers. Crazy or not.

"No, I'm fine." My shaky voice grows stronger with each word.

"Okay. Well, have fun. But like we talked about, not *too* much fun."

She relinquishes the keys to me, but I hold them out to Logan.

Nikki twirls at the door to the Jeep and calls out, "No worries, Aunt O. We have other ideas for a fun night."

Nikki waggles her eyebrows. Aunt Brynna and Aunt Odette glance at each other in one of their weird bestie silent communications that Nikki and I have grown to copy over the years.

"Oh, I don't know if I like that," Aunt Odette mutters to Uncle Christian.

"Nikkola!" Aunt Brynna warns.

Nikki giggles and hops into the backseat in response.

She hands me a CD titled "Homecoming."

"Start with track number two. The Knife will get us in party mode. *And* they match our theme!" She dances away to the band's opening drum solo, shaking the backseat.

"What are you talking about, weirdo?" Laurel asks her, and then shakes her head. "Actually, I don't even care." She slips her earbuds in and turns the volume of her music up until it's so loud that I can hear distorted bass from the passenger seat.

Logan backs out, and we take off in the streamered nightmare of a Jeep that looks like a party supply store barfed all over it.

CHAPTER 7

*W*e pull into the crowded lot of Havenwood Falls High as the sky takes on a beautiful shade of watercolor spill.

"I still don't see why Logan and I had to lie about our costumes. It's not like *we* are the ones doing anything crazy," I grumble from the passenger seat, massaging my temples. My head has throbbed ever since the flashes of light from the cameras.

Nikki leans forward so that she can whisper-hiss past Laurel. "Because your aunt and my mom share a brain. I'm telling you, they would've seen your weird little number and known that what I had planned was epically worse."

We both glance over at Laurel to make sure she isn't listening. She is still lost in her own world, head leaning against the window as she listens to her music.

"Is it hard for you to walk?" Logan asks, waving at a couple of guys from the football team while pulling into a spot.

Nikki wrinkles her nose. "Well, these shoes aren't the comfiest. Why? You offering to carry me, Princess?"

"No, not your shoes. It's amazing that you can even stand upright with a head as big as yours," Logan counters.

"Heavy is the head that wears the crown." Nikki winks at him, and one corner of his mouth turns up.

"I love your confidence, girl." I smile.

Nikki was devastated when she didn't win Teen Miss Havenwood Falls. Up until a few months ago, she was involved in every charity cause to help the town, so she really thought she had a chance at winning. Even though she was nominated, she lost, and it crushed her. Back in September, our friend Paisley helped me start an underground campaign to try to drum up votes for Nikki and her new-kid boyfriend, which led to their nominations for homecoming queen and king.

"Now, we all know what to do, right?" Nikki asks. "Meet at my gym locker at nine-thirty on the dot."

"Why can't we just get this over with first thing?" Logan asks.

"Because, *obviously*, we will catch everyone more off guard if we do it later," she answers.

"And it gives her a chance to accept her crown." I wink at Logan.

Nikki's face shines with hope. "If I pull that off, it will be one of the only things my Mom and I might have in common."

Her tone is light, but a hint of sadness lingers behind it.

We file out of the Jeep. Laurel removes her earbuds and waves at Turner, who sits in the backseat of a car with a couple of his guy friends, feet hanging out. I narrow my eyes at him.

"Later, dudes," she says and then skips away.

Strobing light, accented by bass, pours from the opened gym doors, pulsating through me as we fall into step with everyone else walking in. Paisley weaves her way to the entrance, her boyfriend Cole by her side. Both are punked out and clad in black leather from head to toe, Paisley's ringlets teased into a blond mop. I wave and move to catch up with her, but they disappear. Nikki's secret-ish homecoming campaign was the last time Paisley and I really spent much time together. It sucks. Especially since this is our last year all together.

Logan takes my hand, leading me into the gym.

I hold his hand for a minute, and then release it, pretending to search for something in my purse, because I don't know what the heck we are doing. Sometimes I let my mind go there and think that we could be together . . . And then I come back to reality and know that I will be leaving, no matter what Aunt Odette says. The last thing I want to do is hurt him and ruin our friendship.

The gym is decked out in black and silver with stars hanging from the ceiling. Glittering lights adorn the walls, giving the gym a dreamy atmosphere. A stage has been assembled and placed against the wall, under the basketball hoop. Star centerpieces and glittery confetti adorn tables covered with black tablecloths.

Nikki glances around and sighs. "They changed the decorations."

"What?" I asked.

"When I was still on the committee, we had a completely different color scheme. I literally spent hours on it." Her chin trembles.

"When you drop out of the dance committee without notice, your ideas get trashed," Zaltana Purser says from behind us, Julianna Fairchild at her side. Both are members of the dance committee. Paisley and I couldn't sway either girl to vote for Nikki because they were too hurt and annoyed by her sudden attitude shift.

"Oh, yeah, let's just dredge *that* body up again." Nikki sniffles.

"You're right, it's pointless. There's clearly no getting through to this 'new and improved' version of you, Nikki. Please give me your tickets," Zaltana says, holding her hand out for them.

The guys fork them over, and then Zaltana turns on her heel, moving to the other end of the ticket table with Julianna.

"Come on, Nik," I say, leading her past the two girls as I throw disappointed looks at them.

Yes, Nikki has completely changed and quit, but I know there's a reason, even if she isn't sharing it. This can't be her new normal.

"Let's dance," she mumbles to Max. He takes her hand, leading her to the dance floor.

Viv Freeman chats with Zara Shannon, off the side of the dance floor. They both wear pastel gowns, covering them from neck to toe, their hair curled and twisted into up-dos with matching baby's breath woven into the braids. They laugh at Mr. Friske, our lanky principal, dancing with poor Ms. Bast, who is clearly super uncomfortable with her situation.

"Frisk-e's getting frisky." Logan snorts.

"You look gorgeous, ladies!" I curtsy toward the two girls, and Viv grins.

"So, uh, what are you supposed to be, Amish?" Logan asks.

Zara pulls an old-fashioned fan out and waves it open. Each slat has a name written on it, and one name only, "Darcy."

"What the heck?" Logan asks.

"Oh, cool! Is that like a dance card? Ah, the Bennet sisters. Very nice twist on the theme!" I say.

I poke Logan in the ribs. "Seriously? 'Darcy' didn't tip you off? *Pride and Prejudice* is only one of my and Nikki's favorite books."

"You know I don't read," he admits as we all crack up.

"Wait . . . was that the one with the zombies?" he asks. "Because I'm pretty sure I saw the movie."

Viv, Zara, and I groan. I wave goodbye to them and make my way toward the drink table next to the stage, Logan in tow, to say hi to Mr. Weaver.

"Andrews, you clean up good!" Mr. Weaver teases Logan, wearing his trademark cords and a sweater.

"Hey! Didn't you get the memo?" I joke. "Where's your costume?"

Mr. Weaver grins. "You're looking at it."

"Well, who are you supposed to be?" Logan asks.

"Who are any of us supposed to be? Aren't we all a little starcrossed at some point? *That* is who I represent. The herd," he says with a bow before ladling cloudy blue punch into cups for us. I wave mine away as Logan accepts his cup.

"Philosophical and handy at a refreshment table. Who knew?" I tease.

Mr. Weaver gives me a look. "And who are you? Wait, let me guess . . . Romeo and Juliet?" He sighs. "Alverson, I have to admit, I'm a little disappointed."

"Well, Mr. Weaver, as you have taught us over the years, not everything is as it seems."

"Intro" by the XX blares through the speakers. Nikki and I connect eyes from across the gym, and I am happy to see she appears to be over her disappointment.

The music moves us toward the dance floor, where we meet. We kick our shoes off toward the wall, and twirl each other.

We giggle, losing ourselves in the beat, not worried about where the guys went, or what anyone else is doing. All fears and concerns melt away. My heart swells with how much I already miss my best friend, when she hasn't even left my side yet for her adventures in Seattle.

The sobering thought stops me in my tracks. Nikki twirls a couple more times and tries to bump butts before realizing that she's now dancing alone.

The song ends, and she leans into me, still giggling. "What is it?"

"I don't want this to be the end," I mumble.

She smiles and tugs at my hair. "Sweetheart, this is just the beginning for us."

"But, you're gonna leave." A song that I don't recognize picks up, forcing me to yell over it to be heard.

Nikki grabs my hand and slips her arm around my waist, twirling and then dipping me. "Actually, *you* are the one who is really leaving. I am just jumping states, while you're going full-blown expatriate."

"About that . . . maybe I don't want to. Maybe Aunt Odette was right."

She stands up and releases me. "It's so loud in here I almost thought I heard you say you've been living a lie for as long as I have known you."

"Nik . . ." I grumble. She twirls me again, picking up her pace to keep in time with the music.

"It's so much more than that," I continue. "I feel like I am drowning in life, it's all moving so fast. Aunt Odette is acting weird, and this necklace keeps burning me . . ."

She raises an eyebrow. "Still?"

"Let me guess. You think I am certifiable now."

She looks at me with such longing it takes my breath away, because I know that look.

"What aren't you saying?" I demand.

She pulls me to the side of the dance floor, away from everyone.

"Let me see the necklace." She holds out her hand.

"Why?"

She shrugs. "You know I'm psychic. I'll scan it or something."

I snort, and then pent-up nervous energy turns into bubbling laughter.

She mimics my laugh and then rolls her eyes. "Very funny. You seemed to listen to that quack at the carnival the other night."

Oh, well. This is better than nothing, I suppose. I reach around to try to unclasp the necklace to hand to her, but it's stuck.

"Ouch!" I cry out as the metal bites into the skin under my nail.

"Here, let me see," she says, turning me around so she can work the clasp. It doesn't budge for her, either.

"Hmm." She muses, stepping to the front of me again so that she can examine the crystal. She places it in her hands and closes her eyes.

"Nik? What the hell are you doing?"

She finally releases her hands, eyes flying open. For a second, I see a mirror image of the fear I have felt toward it, but then she blinks, and it's gone.

"What just happened?" I demand.

She opens her mouth and then lets out a breath. "I am not psychic. That's what happened. Just between us girls, I talk a strong game, but Aunt O scares the bejesus out of me when she's ticked. Maybe don't mess with the clasp too much, in case it breaks. Since that thing is old as sin, and a family heirloom."

"So we're just giving up?" I say. "And since when do you use the word 'bejesus'? Who says that?"

She pats my wrist. "Serena? Just talk to your aunt. About all of this. Okay?"

"But—"

"And for now, please promise me we can live in this moment. I mean *really* live in it? It's our last dance," she says.

"No, there's still the winter formal and prom," I say, bewildered by the sadness in her eyes.

"Well, I meant the last homecoming," she amends, a little too quickly. "You know I am all for girl power, but right now, we have a couple of guys who are checking us out."

Nikki nudges me toward where Max and Logan stand. Logan

mingles with the football team, while Max lingers on the fringe. Logan nods at me and smiles, then turns his attention back to Kase and some other guys from the team.

"I know you think I am beating a dead horse, but I have known you your whole life and you have never been as close to a guy as you are to Logan. Can you please just talk to him and figure out what's going on between the two of you?"

"For the love of—"

"Or don't. You keep saying we are running out of time together, and yet you are wasting your own." She kisses me on the lips and then twirls off into Max's arms, almost knocking him over with her force.

I sigh and plop down on the floor, leaning into the padded wall.

Someone blocks the light in front of me. A hand reaches down, and I blink against the glare around the silhouette.

Logan smiles, the straps of my shoes laced through the fingers of his other hand. "May I have this dance?"

I blink.

He clears his throat. "Well, it's how that Darcy guy would've done it, right?

"Unless he was zombie Darcy. Then it would've been more like 'graawwwrraaarrbrains.'" I claw at the air with my hands.

Logan snorts. "You're deranged."

I take his hand, and he lifts me to my feet, awkwardly pulling me into his arms. His hand slides to my back. We both seem to feel the eyes on us as we look up to face a narrow-eyed Mr. Weaver. Logan raises his hand slightly higher on my back, and Mr. Weaver nods, then moves on with a smile.

"You really are beautiful tonight, you know," Logan whispers, red creeping up through his cheeks in time with his words. "Uh . . . not that you aren't every other day!" He rushes to add.

A corner of my mouth lifts. "You're looking pretty handsome yourself."

He smiles down on me. We sway along with the violin solo of the song that flows around us like wisps of smoke, hazing the rest of the crowd out.

"You know, I don't think I've ever seen you in a suit," I muse.

He laughs, the lights glinting against his teeth. "Well, it's a good thing that pictures were taken, because it's never happening again."

"Oh, yeah?" I tease. "What about when you get married?"

The words tighten my throat, and I instantly dread going there.

He stops dancing for a minute and swallows. "Well, maybe once more—I guess that all depends."

My cheeks flame.

"Rena, I have some things I have to say."

"Logan . . ." I plead.

"No, please. Let me do this before what I am pretty sure the punch was spiked with wears off."

Logan continues to twirl me around in the light—I'm a feather in the eye of a storm.

"I have spent so many years infatuated with you. Your quiet strength, the way you've looked out for your sisters, and cared for your mother. I am sorry for all the things I've said that made you or Nikki feel weird about planning to get out of this town. That was all me and my own issues. You shouldn't feel guilty for having dreams. That's another trait of yours that I have always admired."

I suck in a breath as he dips me.

"Where did you learn how to dance?" is all I can utter, when the better question is, *Where is this coming from?*

He grins, lifting me back up. "YouTube. It's not just good for shirt weaving tutorials, you know," he says with a wink.

I blink fast, because tears form on my eyelashes as he continues.

"Deep down, you're this wild girl that a quiet little town like ours has never been able to contain. I know the last thing you want is a guy whose future runs along a small scale, and I know it's selfish, but as proud as I am of you, I just want to freeze this year. Every moment. That's probably why I have been hard on Nikki with Max. It's all changing too fast. It used to just be the three of us."

"Logan." I exhale, his face moving nearer. My hand goes to his cheek, his nose touching mine.

He whispers, "Infatuation is by its nature a selfish thing, so I know that what I feel for you is love. Despite how I feel, I want you to get out there and see all the sights you want to explore, and have all the experiences you crave. I want you to set the world on fire with your beauty and art . . . What's selfish is that I'll never give up hope that one day, you'll come back, ready to be with me."

"I—"

Logan places his finger softly against my lips. "I know. Like I said, selfish. I also know that you're going to point out the fact that we are only eighteen and I'm being ridiculous. As well as I know you, you know me. I am a creature of habit. I can tell you exactly where I want to be in ten years. I want to have expanded my dad's business and built a cabin that puts even your family's to shame, complete with a studio —all for you. Just a simple life. Here. With you. Babies if you want them, and freedom for you to travel for your art, wherever and whenever."

My steps falter, and he catches me. His arms are steady as always, but his voice breaks. "I've been one of your anchors ever since I can remember. Why can't I remain that for you?"

Tears stream down my cheeks freely, spilling onto his jacket. I glance away, unable to meet his gaze because I see it all. I know he's right. I know that I love him, probably always have. But I don't know what level of love it is that I have for him—or if it matches his for me. That aside, how do I make him see that we are just too different?

"I can't even tell you where I will be in three years, Logan. I haven't seen enough of the world. My wants and opinions are forever changing. How is that fair to you?"

His eyes glisten. "Do you love me?"

"Logan . . ."

He stops carrying us and locks me in place with his open, honest glare. "Do. You. Love. Me? It's a simple question."

I nod, blinking faster.

He smiles and wipes the tears from my cheeks. We slowly sway to the music. "Well, why don't we just focus on the time we have this year? I know what you're scared of, but I will never clip your wings, Serena. Why would I destroy what I love most about you?"

I can't breathe, or think, as his heady scent of home and the trees cocoons me with his sweet words. Everything feels out of place lately, leaving me uneasy. So when he moves in, nose brushing mine, I freeze.

Right before our lips meet, the burning sensation on my chest grows so intense that I shriek. I grip the chain and rip as hard as I can to stop the pain, but, again, the necklace won't budge.

"Serena? What is going on with you?" Logan gasps, his eyes huge.

The music cuts to dead silence, of course. Kids stare at me as Mr. Friske bellows into the microphone. "Time to announce this year's homecoming king and queen!"

The kids closest to us continue to stare, most of them laughing. Everyone claps, and pulled from my dream, I gasp in fear of whatever the hell is happening to me. That, combined with the realization that I was about to lead Logan on in the most epic way so far during our friendship, breaks me away from him. I take my shoes from his hand.

"I'm sorry," I mouth as I flee. I look over my shoulder only once. Logan's crestfallen face and red-rimmed eyes sucker-punch me. As I have just done to him.

CHAPTER 8

*L*uckily, the bathroom is empty. I examine my chest in the mirror. A tiny blister slowly forms in the shape of the crystal. *I knew it wasn't in my head.* Fear coils through my stomach, because this is the first burn that hasn't disappeared.

What does it mean? I lean into the path of the overhead light and twirl the chain of the necklace around, trying to remove the damn thing. Nothing. The clasp won't budge.

Cheering and music swell outside the door as I lean on the sink, feeling even worse for missing what was probably Nikki's crowning glory, if she and Max won.

The door crashes open, and Nikki comes "whooping" into the bathroom, shaking her rear, holding her crown in the air in victory.

"Not that there was ever any doubt, but . . ." She throws a tiara-laden fist pump into the air. "Please tell me you weren't in here the whole time and that you saw it!"

I don't answer, so she swishes over to me, a cloud of taffeta. When she takes in my expression, she drops the tiara on the counter. "What's wrong?"

"It won't come off. It b-burned me!" I stutter, fear and panic taking over. She rushes to my side, placing both of her cool hands on my feverish cheeks.

"Girl, you're on fire," she whispers.

"I know! Look at my chest! Family heirloom or not, help me get this thing off!" I beg.

We both yank on the chain, as hard as we can, without strangling me.

It doesn't budge.

I claw at it, but Nikki grabs my hands. "Whoa, Serena. Stop. You're going to draw blood."

She leans in closer. "Where did you say it burned you?"

I roll my eyes, beyond frustrated with the entire situation. "Right. Here. Under the crystal," I say, pointing at it.

"Uh, I don't see anything," she says quietly.

"No! It happened. I had a blister!" I glance in the mirror, down at the spot that was all but oozing pus moments ago—and seeing only creamy skin. It's not even red.

"What?" I exclaim. "That's impossible."

"Serena, I think we should get you home," Nikki says, giving me the same exact worried tone I have sent her way for months. Aggravated as I am with her in this moment, part of me wants to apologize, because holy hell is that annoying.

"No."

"No, what?" she asks, her eyes wide. She backs away from me a little.

I glance into the mirror, and I can see why she is reacting the way she is. I look like a crazy woman.

"No, you worked really hard on this stupid prank, and I am not leaving," I say.

"Really, it's fine."

"We are doing this," I insist. "I've let enough people down tonight."

"What's that supposed to mean?" she asks, still blinking at me like I am insane.

I wipe my cheeks. "Stuff went down with Logan—I ruined it."

"*What?*"

Someone pounds on the door. "Nik, it's 9:25," Max yells.

"Yeah, just announce that to the entire senior class, smooth guy!" Nikki shouts back, turning to me. "What happened with Logan?"

I grab the sparkling tiara from the counter and place it gently on my best friend's head, then slip my shoes on. "Don't worry about it. Tonight is about fun, right? Last dance and all?"

"We will do whatever you want," Nikki says cautiously, helping me wipe my cheeks. "But I think we should leave. You look like hell."

"Maybe it's just a sign that we should spread some," I say.

"Are you sure? Don't tease me, Alverson," she jokes.

I fist bump her and then lead the way to the door. Max and Logan stand on the other side. Logan refuses to meet my eyes as we all sneak into the girls' locker room and file into stalls to change into our prank costumes.

Nikki helps me convert my strapless white vintage Balenciaga gown that we scored from Callie's, eye-hooking it into a halter-neck. This reveals a hidden layer that we spent months hand-sewing red sequins to, so that it would be Carrie White's bloody prom dress without destroying it.

Nikki fixes her creepy-ass Mrs. Voorhees wig.

"Don't forget this, Carrie!" Nikki says, tossing me her tiara. Max hands Logan his own homecoming crown for Logan's Tommy Ross costume.

"See you on the flip side! Keee, keee, keee, ma, ma, ma." Nikki croaks the *Friday the 13th* line, impersonating Mrs. Voorhees's voice. Then she Frankensteins her arms out, walking backward into the hall. A jumpsuit-clad, hockey-masked Max twirls a fake machete, following her.

Logan comes up to me and offers his arm, still not looking directly at me.

"I just need to use the bathroom. I'll be out in a minute," I whisper.

Logan starts to say something, but stops himself and heads out.

I disappear into a stall, and when I come out, I laugh like a fool. I *would* get my period the day that I am dressed as Carrie White, because why would life provide me with anything less strange. Luckily,

I always have stuff in my purse because I have been waiting for this for-freaking-ever.

With a sigh of relief, because now I can at least let go of my health concerns, I head out into the hall and meet Logan.

"You ready for a bloody good time?" He asks, finally looking at me.

"What?" I snap, cheeks burning.

Logan holds the bucket full of red confetti up (because fake blood has no place on Balenciaga—for once, I think Callie would be proud) and adjusts his own crazy blond curly wig with a crown.

I smile. "Oh, I guess. This is insane."

"Let's just humor Nik one last time," he says. "I've been a dick to her and Max, feel like I owe her this."

It's freaking hard to remain unnoticed, but we somehow manage to sneak under the table next to the makeshift stage undetected.

Artemis, the tech expert from the drama club, meets us to take the bucket of red confetti, quickly rigging it to an impromptu pulley directly above the basketball hoop overhead.

When we hear the *Friday the 13th* theme music and the screams and laughter, we crawl out from under the table and take our places on the stage with our crowns in place.

On cue, red confetti rains down on Logan and me. I glance up, watching it sparkle and tumble down. A hush falls over the crowd. They stare at us, mouths gaping, some laughing. Max, in his Jason mask and with a fake machete, has hacked away at tons of random people, in addition to the ones who signed on to take part, spraying them all with fake blood.

My gaze falls on a familiar pair of eyes in the crowd—sea-glass green, peeking out from under a black hood. The guy who has been chasing me! My heart stutters.

Energy seems to shift, and then release, exploding in a sonic boom through the room, shaking the floor. I look out at the mass chaos ensuing. Kids scream and fall over.

I search for the guy from the cemetery, but he's gone, lost in the crowd.

"Logan?" I scream.

He wraps his arm around me, pulling me from the stage into the corner, covering me with his body.

What the hell? A bomb? That guy? My mind starts going through bad movie plots and flashes of news stories on terrorist attacks and school shootings.

"We have to find Laurel!" I yell over the din.

"I saw her sneak out with Turner over an hour ago. She's gone," Logan yells back to be heard over the crowd. Though I want to choke her for leaving with that loser, I'm relieved she isn't here.

My chest feels lighter, so I glance down. The necklace slowly lifts, the crystal floating before it's somehow jerked off my neck and disappears. *But how?* A strange metallic clink echoes throughout the gym. Looking around me, I note other pieces of jewelry scattered on the gym floor.

A bunch of football players and cheerleaders flee out the open door, into the night. *What the hell? Did they do this?*

I look at Logan and see my own fear and confusion reflected as the floor shakes again.

"We have to get out of here!" Logan yells.

Someone I don't really know stands at the edge of a group of kids. His body contorts at strange angles, like his bones are breaking and reforming in a new shape.

When he looks up, his eyes glow and his teeth grow into jagged points. I scream, pulling Logan toward the exit.

Mr. Friske yells something in a weird language. Everything falls silent. I turn to Logan to figure out why the hell he isn't moving with me and find him frozen in place.

"Logan?" I ask.

No response.

"Logan!" I scream.

Other kids are paralyzed, like he is, but not everyone. Zaltana stares over at me wide-eyed and then I see Nikki, blinking in shock.

I run over to her. "Logan—something is wrong with him."

"Max, too," Nikki whispers.

Within what feels like seconds, adults filter into the gym in silence. "What's going on?" I demand. "Shouldn't the sheriff be here?"

A well-dressed, dark-haired man steps forward—Roman Bishop. My legs turn to jelly, and not in a good way. I don't know him personally, only the stories I have heard. He is one of the most powerful men in our town. *What the heck is he doing here?*

Addie Beaumont whisks in behind Roman wearing knee-high boots, torn jeans, and a leather jacket. A sense of comfort and familiarity rush over me. On occasion, we chat in line at Coffee Haven, and she's even bought some of my jewelry.

"Addie? What's happening?" My voice breaks.

She shakes her head at me and Nikki, her dark glasses framing the annoyance flashing in her eyes.

Addie's assistant, Athena Lawrence, hisses. "Why did I know that this reeked of Nikkola? And you, Serena, what kind of friend are you to allow something so idiotic?"

"I—I don't understand," I say.

Nikki weaves her fingers through mine. "Addie, I'm sorry. This was my fault. Not Serena's."

Addie grabs Nikki's free hand, wrenching her free from me as she sets her down in a chair. Addie unwraps what looks like a tattoo kit.

Nikki's eyes widen. "What are you doing?"

My throat tightens. "Hey, what's going on? Are you giving her a tattoo? But . . . *why?*"

"We understand your concern, Serena, but you need to stay out of this. Why don't you go wait outside?" Athena murmurs. "Nikkola, please sit still. We don't want to hurt you."

Addie lines up different inks on a table, and Nikki struggles to break free from the arms that hold her down.

"There was clearly just some sort of a terrorist attack, and now you are giving a kid a *tattoo*? It makes no sense!" I yell.

"Please, Mr. Friske! I'm sorry!" Nikki howls in the principal's direction, but he turns away.

"Wait! Shouldn't her parents be here?" I demand.

"They're on the way, child." A raspy voice, evil as sin, fills the room. Ada Daryn, a blue-eyed brunette with an old-Hollywood vibe, who looks decades too young to be Stella's mom and Ellisyn's grandmother, struts toward us.

"Since they are not here to claim Nikkola, I act as guardian. Emergency contact and all," she says, flashing me a strange smile.

"No, my aunt is Nikki's emergency contact," I argue.

"Please do what you need to teach this young witch to mind her place," Ada snaps at Addie and Athena.

"What?" I gasp. Then I let out a nervous laugh. "Oh! Nikki, you got us all good. You were right! This is the most epic senior prank ever." I laugh until Ada clears her throat.

"Are you quite finished with your hysterics, or must I slap you?" She turns from me and returns to Nikki. "I am disgusted by this utter waste of your talent. You are officially warned."

Ada waves to Addie to continue whatever it is that Addie is doing, and then makes her way over to me, leaning in.

"My dear, you are absolutely on the cusp." Ada pats my cheek. Her eyes alight, she pivots, narrowing them at Roman Bishop as she bumps him roughly with her shoulder before she exits.

"What does she mean you're a witch?" I ask Nikki, who won't look at me.

Anger shoots into my veins—real and primal. A live wire entrapped. My entire body burns. I cry out and start to go down to the floor. Mr. Weaver suddenly appears at my side, holding me up.

"Alverson, you okay? You don't look so hot," he says, concern lining his forehead.

"I—I don't know. Can you please explain any of this?" I wrench myself free of him when Nikki screams.

"My powers!" she sobs. "Addie, why!"

What powers?

Athena sighs. "I'm sorry, Nikkola. It was decided by the Court. You have a temporary restraint on all magic until you appear before them."

"What is going *on?*" I yell. No one answers, but Mr. Weaver quietly shushes me.

Nikki's tears fall onto the birdcage tattoo that Addie formed on Nikki's chest, near her heart.

I rush to her side. "Nikki, I am so confused," I whisper.

She cries into my arms, and the painful current rips through me again. I lose my footing once more, but she catches me.

"Serena?" Nikki gasps.

Roman Bishop steps to the center of the room and thunders, "What was seen here tonight will only be remembered by the few who hear me speaking. You have a responsibility to keep it to yourselves. Any who abuse their power, or break this gag order, will be dealt with. As Nikkola Morris will be. We are better than this, kids. Remember that."

A young woman I don't recognize appears at Roman's side and whispers something.

"The wards are back up and stronger this time, to prevent another ill-conceived prank," Roman says to Principal Friske, who nods. Whatever that means . . .

One by one, the adults filter out as quickly as they came.

My body buzzes with restless energy. My mind is on a nonstop loop, trying to make sense of everything.

"What did Roman mean, we have a 'responsibility'? And what was Ellisyn's grandmother talking about? I mean, I know we joked about it when we were little, but there's no such thing as witches," I say to Nikki. "Right?"

Before she can answer, Aunt Brynna and Uncle Christian arrive, their ashen faces set in stone as they cart her away from me without even saying hello.

"No! Serena needs me!" Nikki screams.

"Nikki, why? Tell me what you know!" I cry after her.

Once Nikki leaves, the music starts back up, and the frozen kids all break free, moving around, laughing and poking fun at Max in his costume. Like nothing ever happened.

From the rambling, it appears they only remember him running through in costume, and nothing of the strange happenings that took place after. A few kids who weren't frozen look at me with solemn, knowing looks. I start to make my way over to them, but then Logan is at my side, laughing.

"That was hilarious." He pats Max on the shoulder as Max pulls his mask off, all sweaty and grinning.

"Where's Nik?" Max asks.

I swallow hard, trying to work through the buzzing energy swarming my body, doing my best to hide what really happened. Ridiculous as this all is, Roman Bishop scares the crap out of me, and something tells me not to cross him.

"Uh, her parents heard about the prank and came to pick her up. They were pissed. Think she's grounded." Pain shoots through my body, and I wince.

"Serena, do you have any one who can pick you up? I think you need to go home and rest," Mr. Weaver says, looking at me in a strange way. Only now do I realize that he has never left my side.

"Rena, you okay?" Logan asks.

The painful buzzing in my body is so bad I can't even answer for a minute.

"I can take her home, Mr. Weaver. I drove her here." Logan volunteers.

Mr. Weaver nods, and I lean into Logan as he leads me out. When my legs buckle once more, he picks me up and carries me to the Jeep.

CHAPTER 9

After an uncomfortably silent ride home, the conversation we had at the dance a silent passenger, we pull into my driveway.

"Thanks for driving, and for this." I hold my wrist up, playing with the red petals of the roses on my corsage. My body throbs as I slowly make my way out of the Jeep.

"Hey, easy!" Logan says, rushing from the driver's side to the passenger side to help me. Once the pain lessens, I test standing on my own, and he cautiously sets me free in front of my darkened house.

Laurel must still be out with Turner. Simon and Lena will still be in Grand Junction for a few hours at least, and who knows where Aunt Odette is.

Another volt of pain shoots through my body, and I cry out and fall.

"Serena! Seriously, do you need a doctor or something?"

"Logan, please go home. I think I just need to go to bed."

"No." Concern thickens his voice. "Look, I know I overstepped tonight, and I'm sorry if it made you uncomfortable. But I'm not sorry I told you the truth. And I want to make sure you are okay."

I push myself to my feet and nod. "I'm sorry for my reaction—I just have a lot on my plate right now and feel like I got hit by a truck. Maybe I'm getting some weird zombie flu."

He doesn't appear convinced. My cheeks flush with fever, and every cell of my body trembles. Am I allergic to these changes in my body? That must be it.

Or maybe the adults did something to me in the gym. If they said Nikki is a witch, what the hell are *they*?

A wave of nausea hits me as phantom currents and flames lick at my limbs.

I look over my shoulder toward the waterfall, glittering in the half-moon like a light tower directing me home. Tears sting my eyes, and a breath catches in my throat. I've grown up looking at it my whole life, without really seeing each facet—the most beautiful thing . . .

"Hey, why are you crying?" Logan's voice loses all mirth.

Ignoring him, I follow my body's pull to the water.

"Uh, are we going swimming? In our clothes, on a freezing night, Crazy?" Logan asks, pulling me out of my head. The gentle current of water teases my toes, kissing them, as I stand in the rocky sand and twigs.

"No, of course not. It's just . . . soooobeautifuulllll." Sobs cut me off, and his arms are around me.

"Uh . . . hey, we've done crazier," he says, using his thumb to wipe a tear from my cheek. Electricity zaps me, and I flinch away. Logan pulls back, wide-eyed.

"Did you feel that?" I gasp.

He blinks and flashes a weak excuse of a cover-up grin. "Happens to me all the time with the ladies. I say let's go for a dip if it will make you feel better."

The woodsy musk that has always been Logan's, and usually calms me, takes on a rancid twist for a split second. The thrumming in my body picks up, and I wince. Then he smells amazing again.

"Rena?" Logan asks, eyeing me. His lips are right there, like they were before everything went so horribly wrong. This time I want them in a way I never really allowed myself to in the past. All the questions and complications I created for us in my head seem like a faraway dream.

"I know what will make me feel better." I lean into him, grabbing his face.

Logan sucks in a breath and then pulls me into his arms.

I don't know who initiates it, but our lips whisper across each other. Not gently like the books describe, but with a burning that rivals the forging current that continues to ravage my body.

He trails his lips down my neck, whispering in my ear. "I've waited for this since like sixth grade."

I shake my head as he returns to me, smiling into his lips. Then we are in the water, my gown billowing around me. Logan's suit jacket is long gone. He breaks the kiss, to my frustration, and then his shirt slips over his head.

His scent even stronger, I'm drawn to his neck, trailing kisses down it as we move deeper into a cool spot.

The waterfall roars in the background. I can hear every single drop cascade down to her sisters, pooling around us. Everything feels lighter, and the buzzing bolts of pain leave my body. I raise my head to let out a sigh of relief.

When I move back to his neck, nothing is enough. My jaw hurts. I screech as tiny knives cut though my gums. *The pressure.* I just need to bite down.

His carotid pulses, and it's delicious.

Mine.

He's putty in my hands, and before I know what I'm doing, my teeth sink into his neck.

Logan cries out as sweet blood rushes into my mouth like the juice of a peach.

But it's not a peach. It's Logan's flesh. Logan's blood. My best friend, who is no longer pulling me toward him, or reacting in any way. He stills in my arms. Save for the buoyancy afforded by the water, I would never be able to support him like this.

Tiny bolts of electricity fire from my body, shooting into his under the water like little veins of a monster, and I scream.

"Logan?"

His eyes stay focused on mine, frozen in accusatory terror, as he floats in my arms.

I retch into the water next to me, coughing up his blood.

Blood. That I consumed.

Red droplets spider-web around rose petals knocked loose from my corsage, in a macabre two-step.

A wail tears from my lungs, but then it turns into a foreign laugh as the water rocks through me, a cooling salve to my searing worries. My tongue examines the tiny layer of daggers shielding my teeth.

The water trickles around, whispering in the same voice as the whisper in my dream on my birthday:

You're helping Logan, Serena. Water is birth. Water is life. Water is death.

Memories from over the years, of Aunt Odette and Mama, surrounded by countless floating dead men and lightning bolts striking under the surface, assail me, as though unlocked in my mind. I glance down and see my reflection—the smirking girl in the water.

His warm blood calls to me, so I dive back in to cut the remaining strands of life force clinging to Logan's feeble body.

CHAPTER 10

"*S*ERENA, STOP!" someone screams from the shore. Suddenly, Aunt Odette is by my side. I'm shaking and dry heaving, and the buzz that left my body returns to my head and ears. My hand flies to my mouth when my gums are cut through once more, as the sharp teeth retract. I can see my aunt's lips moving, but can't make out the words as she pulls us to shore. Once on land, the buzz dulls enough that I can hear her.

"Get me a blanket." Aunt Odette's voice is calm and measured as it breaks through my hysteria.

"I don't know what happened . . . I—"

Her blue eyes flash. "Blanket. NOW."

I scramble to my feet. The weight of waterlogged gravity pulling on my dress causes me to stumble. I right myself and then run into the house, sliding on the hardwood floor and banging my thigh into the wall, but I barely register it.

I killed him.

I kissed my best friend, then bit his neck and killed him. *Who. Does. That!*

I grab the quilt from my bed and race back to her side.

"Should I call 911?" I gasp, my voice tiny as I picture a jail cell with no windows. Not that it matters, if he's dead. Nothing does. They can stick me anywhere.

"No." She drips a handful of water over Logan's neck, and the puncture wounds close, fading to nothing in front of my eyes. I let out a loud sob, and she yanks me to her side, covering my mouth.

"I know this is overwhelming, but pull it together, girlfriend."

I obey, and she slides over to make room for me, while putting an ear to his mouth and gently grasping his wrist to feel his vein.

"Sweetie, he's breathing. He just has a weak pulse. That can easily be remedied, once you return what belongs to him."

"What?"

She puts her hands on my shoulders. "Do you trust me?"

I nod without having to think about it. She nods back and positions my head over his. "Breathe into him."

I do what she says, and my throat closes. I'm choking, but nothing is in my mouth for me to choke on.

Aunt Odette holds me down, even when I try to pull away. "Fight through it, sweet pea. It will pass."

And she's right. Whatever it was moves from me into him. But nothing happens.

The numbness I had taken for granted in my body while in the water switches back to the thrumming, pent-up energy, but it's not as bad as it was. Really, when your friend is lying in front of you, possibly dying, your own pain means nothing.

"Come on, damn it!" Aunt Odette growls, pounding on his chest once. Logan's body seizes and stills. And then he coughs.

"Logan?" I choke through my tears and pull back, partially to give him some air, but mostly because I no longer trust myself anywhere near him.

He opens his eyes, dazed at first, and then terror returns to them. Logan has never looked at me like this before, and it kills me. His hand rushes to this throat and he tries to skitter away.

But Aunt Odette pins him down. Her eyes glow, locking on his as she whispers in a foreign language. A flashback of countless versions of Aunt Odette, whispering to me in that same language over the years, eyes glowing, bombards me.

It doesn't make sense to my ears, but my brain understands what she's saying to him, and he settles down.

Aunt Odette continues in English. "Shhhh, it's okay! You fell into the lake and hit your head, Logan. Serena and I pulled you out."

He blinks, glancing back and forth between the two of us. *He will never buy it.*

"You." His voice is accusatory as he focuses on me. Then I realize that must've just been in my head, because his voice is soft. He whispers, "You saved me."

Tears stream down my cheeks. I shake my head, and Aunt Odette firmly grabs my shoulders.

Nails digging into them, she says, "She's being humble. Serena dragged you out of that water like it was nothing, Logan. You will be just fine, aside from whatever you swallowed."

He laughs, along with her hollow laugh. I can't stop crying.

"Hey," he says, pushing up on an elbow. "It's okay, I'm here. We can go back in."

"No!" This time it's me scrambling to get away from him. I run into the house as I hear Aunt Odette's soothing tone out in the yard with Logan.

I lock myself in the bathroom, the humming of my body so intense that I just need quiet. Remembering how the water helped, I fill the tub and sit on the side of it, leaning over the toilet just in time for the rest of my dinner to make its exit when the metallic aftertaste of Logan's blood lurches my stomach into action.

"Serena? Serena, let me in," Aunt Odette demands.

"Sick." I gag on the word.

She sighs. "Are you going to be okay if I drive Logan home?"

I murmur a lie.

"Don't you dare leave. I think we both know how badly you and I need to talk." She lingers a moment, and then her footsteps fade away.

I flush the toilet and then strip down and get into the full tub.

The water doesn't have the same effect that the lake did, but a bath is a bath. My tears drip into the water as I set my head back and try to relax. *He's okay.*

But I'm not. Every time I close my eyes, I relive it. The horror in

Logan's eyes, his limp body, the blood. How some strange part of me reveled in it.

Me. The girl who can't even handle the thought of eating a cheeseburger.

I lower my head in shame, and a flash bleats through my closed eyes. I glance down to see tiny currents of lightning shoot upward from my submerged body to the surface of the water.

Just like with Logan.

I suck in a breath, blink, and it's gone.

I scramble to free myself of the tub, grabbing my robe from behind the door. I wrap it around myself, tears streaming down my cheeks as I rip the door open.

"Aunt Odette?" I yell.

Nothing.

She must not be back from taking Logan home yet.

Logan. The tears come harder when I remember him, lifeless, floating in the water.

Fear of this body I'm trapped in propels my feet up two flights of stairs, to my first home.

"Mama?" I choke on the word, clearing the room until I am at her side.

"Mama, I don't know what's happening to me."

She stares out the window, eyes vacant.

Anger over how my sisters and I have been robbed by losing both Mama and Daddy pulsates through my body, my fists balling at my sides.

"I need you, Mama."

No response. And that is my undoing.

I have tried to be strong over the years. Aunt Odette was there for us, making sure we were loved and cared for. But that has never erased the pain and grief of the absence of my parents. And now this—whatever this is—not having my Mama to help me through . . .

I crumble, anger deflating itself back into a bone-crushing grief. My body folds into the tiny space between Mama and the side of her chair as I curl up against her, like I used to when I was a little girl. My damp hair and tears dot the front of her nightgown. I feel like a jerk for soaking her clothes, but I just need her.

"Mama, I'm a monster," I whisper.

"No, Serena. You are magnificent." Aunt Odette's voice fills the room.

I turn around, wiping my tears to find my aunt in the doorway, light from the hallway haloing her.

"What?"

"Sweetie, you and I need to talk," Aunt Odette says, coming forward to help me off Mama.

I hesitate, glaring at my aunt, fear icing my spine when I see the look on my aunt's face—reverent. *But I almost killed someone.*

"What is wrong with you?" I shout, lowering my voice when Mama tenses against my side.

She sighs. "Serena, let me change your mother into dry clothes, and then I think we should take this somewhere else."

She nods toward Mama's rigid body. I rise to my feet, not wanting to upset Mama further, and realizing how selfish I was to get that close to her without knowing what is going on with me.

What if I hurt her, too?

My hands fly over Mama, checking for any damage. Then I remember that my hands are part of me, of this body—which is apparently a lethal weapon.

Biting my lip, I turn and flee to my room. I shut the door and curl up in the window seat facing the falls. As much as I don't want to look, I cannot deny the pull. It's not so much that my body wants to be in the water, but it feels like the water has claimed me. When I focus hard enough, I can still hear whispers woven into the ever-present clamorous rush of the falls.

"Baby girl, we should have talked a long time ago," my aunt says, stepping into my room. "Simon told me, but I didn't listen . . ." she adds, an afterthought.

This admission fans the flames of my anger anew.

I whirl to my feet, facing her. "You knew this would happen? And you told *Simon* instead of me, first? What am I? Why does the necklace you gave me keep burning me? Did you do this to me? Why did I almost kill Logan?" My voice breaks, but I continue. "Why does my body feel like this? God, I just want to crawl out of my skin."

Now that my mind is focusing on it, the buzzing grates on me, not quite painful any more. It's more like the pent-up energy of a limb that has lost circulation. Annoying, demanding attention. Only, unlike a foot that has fallen asleep, there is no explanation for this.

She drops onto my bed, eyes glazing. "The necklace, of course! Serena, where is it?" Her voice raises in alarm.

"I don't know. There was an explosion or something at the dance, and right after it happened, the necklace fell off. Which makes no sense, because I couldn't remove it, no matter how hard I tried. It kept burning me, ever since the night you gave it to me."

"Why didn't you tell me?" she demands.

I snort. "Oh, yeah, because that's totally an easy and rational conversation for me to have with you. 'Thanks for the necklace, not so crazy about the burns, though.'"

"Serena, you know you can talk to me about anything."

I narrow my eyes. "Do I? Because last I checked, you still haven't told me what's wrong with me, or why you're being so calm about the fact that I almost killed my best friend, and that you were able to stop it."

My heart stutters as I remember her eyes glowing, the weird language she spoke when calming Logan, and seemingly making him forget the whole ordeal. The weird déjà vu slams into me—Aunt Odette and Mama, surrounded by dead men in the water.

"Aunt Odette—what are *you*?"

She sits up straighter, appearing almost regal, even though her eyes remain sad.

"Serena, you need to know something first. They don't choose just anyone for an honor like this—we Alverson women are special."

"You and Mama, you're murderers. I was almost a murderer," I rasp.

"No," she says firmly. "We are not murderers, any more than God is. And tonight . . . well, that never should have happened. We need to find your necklace as soon as possible."

"What the hell does that matter right now?" I cry out, pacing in frustration at Aunt Odette's strange half-answers.

Her face pales. "That necklace is everything."

"Wait—can you just tell me what the hell we are, first?"

"Honey, I know this is scary and overwhelming, but there are a lot of moving parts in this explanation. I need you to sit down."

"No! You don't get to call the shots this time, Aunt Odette. I'm sorry, I love you, but—"

"Serena. Give her a chance." Simon's figure darkens my doorway.

He turns to my aunt. "I came as quickly as I could."

"Where's Lena?" Aunt Odette asks, panicked.

"She's reading, in the tavern. Don't worry," Simon reassures her.

Lena. Laurel.

"Is this going to affect them, too?" I ask, worry for my baby sisters trumping my own concerns.

Aunt Odette nods. "Now you see why we need that necklace."

"Actually, I don't. Because all I know is that it hurt me."

"The necklace is special. It has been in the family since we were first honored by this calling. Josie Alverson, the first siren, wore it into Havenwood Falls."

"So, we're sirens?" I ask, trying to rack my mind for anything I have ever read or watched on the topic, but nothing comes to me.

That superior look returns to her face. "Yes. When Havenwood Falls first formed, it was meant to be a haven for certain types—supernatural beings."

If this conversation happened a week ago, I would have laughed. But after what I witnessed tonight . . .

"Wait, Nikki really is a witch, then?" I ask.

"Yes."

"You knew? All these years, you knew that about Nikki, and me. You didn't tell me any of this?"

"Honey, I thought I was protecting you. The necklace is important because it is a form of training wheels for a new siren, so to speak. It reins your power in and controls the discomfort you feel when away from the water, until your body can learn to regulate its new normal.

Your body prepares to siren as you prepare for your first period. I take it that happened tonight?" she asks.

My cheeks flame, and I don't meet Simon's eyes. Something tells me he is probably as interested in the floor right now as I am.

"Why is Simon here? No offense, Simon. Why does he know about us?"

Aunt Odette smiles up at Simon, whom I finally bring myself to glance at for a split second. He smiles down at her so lovingly that it's nauseating.

"Because he saw me for what I was and gave me a chance. Which is what I am begging of you right now."

"Would it help if I told you that I had a secret, too?" Simon asks.

I shrug, secretly curious, not sure if I even want to know.

"I'm a dragon shifter."

I snort, and then laughter erupts until I can't breathe.

"Right," I say between laughs. "That's enough *Final Fantasy* for you."

He feigns hurt. "Uh—my alter ego is way better than yours, so . . ."

This only makes me laugh harder, until his words pull me back to my own reality.

"Oh, God. This is real?" My head spins so I fold over, putting it between my knees, like my aunt used to tell me to do when I would get car sick.

"She's actually taking this a lot better than I thought she would," Simon murmurs under his breath.

"Honey?" Aunt Odette asks, bracelets jangling as she comes to my side.

I take a few deep breaths and then look toward the waterfall. The sight of it takes the edge off the nausea. When I watch the water froth and dance, something subconsciously comforts me. *This is right. Of course, it is.* Water has always been my haven.

"Is anyone in this town actually human?" I ask, keeping my eyes on the falls.

"Well, yeah, of course," Simon answers.

"Logan . . ." I say. "He's human, right?"

"And until we find your necklace, and get you fully trained, you must stay away from him, and other human men." Aunt Odette says.

"Why only men?" I ask, almost wanting to kick myself for my own stupidity, because it was only dead men that I saw in the flashes of Mama and Aunt Odette in the water.

"Mama was in the water at the Carnival the other day!" I say.

"Yes," Aunt Odette answers, carefully.

"How? She can't move."

"You're going to have to trust the limits of what I tell you for now. All I can say is that the siren in her is stronger than the prison she has built in her mind. I mostly handle the requirements the town has for the sirens on my own. There are usually three at a time, and always three Alverson sisters in each generation. Now that you are going to join me, it will help. We hold a massive harvest on October eleventh, every year. Your mother's pull to siren and the magic from the town allow her to step out of her own head to fulfill her responsibility on that night."

"What about her responsibility to us?" I whisper.

"Believe me, when she has a moment of clarity on that day each year, she begs me to fill her in on what is happening with all three of you. The hard part is that she forgets as soon as she remembers your father's death, and then goes back into herself. We have to start over again the next year."

My chin trembles. "She never wanted to see us on that day? I know I have gotten close a few times. You did something to me. I remember it."

"I had to wipe your memories of it, Serena. Those wipes are losing hold because you are transforming, so the repressed memories are returning."

"Why?"

"I told you I wanted to protect you. All those years that your period didn't come. The doctors told me you might be sterile."

"They never told me that."

"I asked them not to, while you were a minor. It was so hard. Part of me was excited that you might be the first of our kind to be able to get away and escape this. While it is an honor to protect our home, it comes at a dear price."

It suddenly hits me. "This is why you didn't want me to plan on college overseas."

Tears glimmer in her eyes. "Oh, baby, I wanted it for you," she cries. "I want the world for you, and deep down, I hoped. I came in here, so many nights after you fell asleep, laying the crystal of that necklace on your chest, to see if it reacted, but it never did. That lulled me into a false sense of security. I knew that you were going to Europe, at least for a few weeks this summer, so it was time to give you the necklace, as a precaution. I swear I was going to talk to you before you left. The first time it activates, sensing that you are close to sirening, it lights up the night."

I snort. "Yeah, I know. That happened after you went to bed, on my birthday . . ."

"When you went swimming," she finishes. "I should have known. God, I have failed you. I am sorry for that. I just wanted to keep hope alive that you could break free, but I didn't want to overly encourage a shining future that I wasn't sure you would be able to have."

"Why can't I just leave? I don't want this. I can't even stand to eat a chicken nugget, and you expect me to fry men and then drink their blood?"

"The blood part isn't totally necessary," Simon answers.

"You will get that under control." Aunt Odette tries to reassure me.

"No, I don't want to get it under control. I don't want this. What if I just leave?"

Aunt Odette sets her jaw. "You die. Or you end up like your mother."

My lungs refuse to expand as that punch lands in my gut. *She tried to leave us?* I don't remember that.

"If you remove yourself from your water source," Aunt Odette says, pointing to the falls, "the imbalanced electrons in your body will fry you."

"The buzzing?"

"Yes, that is a store of electricity that your body maintains to paralyze your victim in the water. It's like venom, in a sense. I know it sounds horribly inhumane, but it is painless. The current in the water paralyzes them, while we get to play out their deathbed fantasy. Clearly, you have always been Logan's. So that is what he saw."

My cheeks burn, and I hurry to change the subject. "So, I should stay away from Simon, too?"

"Nope. And that's why I told you the truth about what I am, Serena. You're not alone in this. And you can't hurt me. Well, I mean, you can *try*," he teases.

"We only Harvest human men that the Court and the covens overseeing town ask us to harvest," Aunt Odette says, rolling her eyes at Simon with a tiny smile.

"Why would they ask us to do something so terrible?" My mind goes back and forth from instinctively accepting this as right, because an ancient level of my subconscious already knew that this was my path, to the other part of me that bucks against it all in horror.

"Serena, this town is full of unique types who have been hunted since the beginning of time. Every so often hunters, or other humans with evil intentions, come to town and need to be dealt with. The town has magical wards, put in place by the Luna Coven, overseen by the Court of the Sun and the Moon. These wards help protect us, but occasionally someone bad gets through, and that is where we come in."

"We have covens?"

Aunt Odette smiles. "Surely, you didn't think Nikki was the only one of her kind? I know you saw some interesting things at the dance tonight. Brynna called before you came home."

"Are Addie and Roman a part of either of those groups?"

"Both are major players, actually. Why?"

"They were at the school tonight after everything happened."

"Honey, they were there to keep you guys safe. Before any of the supe kids accidentally hurt each other, or a human."

"Is Nikki okay? Everyone seemed really mad at her." Guilt tears through me for not having asked about her sooner and being so wrapped up in my own drama.

Aunt Odette winces. "Yeah, you won't be seeing much of Miss Nikki for a while."

"Is she grounded?" I ask.

Simon clears his throat.

"Honey, Nikki used her magic to breach the wards that the Luna Coven placed on your school. She is in very, very big trouble, and stands to lose all of her powers permanently."

"But, that doesn't sound like Nikki!" I argue.

"Serena, please don't take this the wrong way, but it might be time for you to entertain the fact that you don't know the real Nikki as much as you thought you did," Simon quietly advises.

"No! I know her better than anyone . . ." But the argument sounds weak even to my own ears. How well do I really know this girl I have shared so much of my life with? An image from the dance flashes in my mind and doesn't help.

"I saw a kid start to change into something else, Aunt Odette." I shudder. "It was horrible. Was it because Nikki dropped the . . . wards? Is that what you called them?"

Aunt Odette moves over to my side and wraps her arms around me.

"Yes, sweetie. It was a very foolish and dangerous thing for her to do. I know this is a lot to digest, and I know it isn't fair. I'm sorry. Please just know that even with the supernatural, there is a natural order to things. We coexist pretty well, most of us more peaceful than most of the human world outside our borders. When beings have been oppressed for centuries, they tend to be more sensitive to attaining peace, and then preserving it."

"But, I don't want to hurt anyone . . ." A memory of a man floating in the water at the most recent Carnival this week stops me.

"What is it?" Aunt Odette asks.

"Dr. Nance! I saw Mama take him down. Why? He was good. He helped me when I was little."

Simon works his jaw and crosses his arms over his broad chest.

"He was a sick man. He experimented on supes in his free time," Aunt Odette explains.

"There have been a few murders that were traced back to him. The police found evidence of tortured supernatural beings." Simon growls.

I cannot seem to pull enough air in, and scrub my face with my hands, to get rid of the tingling before I completely hyperventilate.

"So, a doctor is bad, but we are good for killing him?"

"No, not killing. Harvesting. We harvested his life force, merging it with the magical properties of the water in our falls, then we siphoned what is needed to help sustain the town's wards. Serena, we are the only ones in this town with the ability to turn pure evil into good. We are the silent guardians of our home, protecting everyone we love and care for. When we take the lives the Court asks us to, it's only after all the major figures in this town have exhausted all other choices for the individual—they are that dangerous. When we harvest them, they aren't even in pain. Compare that with the human form of the death sentence . . ."

"Logan was terrified!" I argue.

"Because you don't know what you are doing yet. I will teach you, and then, together, we will teach Laurel and Lena, so that the three of you can take over when my time, and your mother's, has passed."

My throat tightens, and my heart pounds. "No, not them."

Aunt Odette squeezes me. "I felt the same way for Karina, and your mother felt the same about the two of us, at first. It is completely natural as a big sister. But it's this or death. There's no way around it."

Aunt Odette glances up to Simon. "We need to find her necklace. She can't leave the house without it until we get her under control."

"I was at the school already and haven't seen it. Friske is on high alert for it, though. He will call as soon as he finds it. Multiple pieces were lost tonight," Simon says.

I have received so many answers that one of the more important things nagging at me has been neglected, and now comes bobbing to the surface of my mind. Sea-glass eyes. A hood. *He* was at the dance.

"Oh!"

"What?"

"There's something else. Simon, that guy, he is still following me. I think I saw him at the dance, right before the explosion."

Aunt Odette and Simon exchange the same look of pure panic.

"You don't think . . . How could they already track her? She's so new," Aunt Odette says.

"I never put anything past their kind." Simon spits the words out. "I'm on it." He disappears before I can say anything.

"What's wrong now?" I ask.

Aunt Odette doesn't meet my eyes. "It's nothing."

"No! Stop lying to me. Please."

"Simon told me about the guy in the cemetery."

"Narc," I mutter.

"No. He did the right thing. I told you how we take out hunters, right?"

My lungs freeze.

"Well, sometimes they have vengeful friends."

"I saw him by the water at the carnival! I am almost positive. I think he was holding a knife, and he was looking at you and Mama."

She purses her lips into a white line, the color draining from her cheeks.

"He was that close to you that many times?" she whispers.

I shrug.

"I'm going to go grab your sisters and call for backup. For now, do not leave this room. Stay away from the window and get dressed in case we have to move quickly." She tilts her head. "Do you think you could draw a picture of him for me?"

I nod, trying to swallow past the lump in my throat. *How do I go from being the unlikely hunter to the hunted within one night?*

She touches my cheek, her face lined with worry. "I know I threw a lot at you. I promise, I will be right here, helping you through it all. I will tell you as much as I can. There is going to be some stuff I must keep from you for a bit still, and I know that pisses you off. I get it. But please trust me. Other than this, have I ever let you down?"

I glance into her eyes, remembering the illnesses she lost sleep over, taking care of me, the baked cookies, the blanket forts, the stories, the endless supply of love and selflessness.

"I trust you, but please, no more secrets."

She kisses my forehead, then hurries out of my room, digging her cell phone from her pocket. Her voice carries down the stairs.

I slip into sweatpants and a hoodie, and then sit down at my desk, opening my colored pencils.

My fingers shake as the pale green eyes, peeking out from underneath a black hood, come to life in front of me.

Eyes belonging to a man who wants to kill me and my family.

~

WATCH for the sequel to *The Fall*, coming April 6, 2018.

We hope you enjoyed this story in the Havenwood Falls High series of novellas featuring a variety of supernatural creatures. The series is a collaborative effort by multiple authors. Each book is generally a stand-alone, so you can read them in any order, although some authors will be writing sequels to their own stories. Please be aware when you choose your next read.

OTHER BOOKS in the Young Adult Havenwood Falls High series:
Written in the Stars by Kallie Ross
Reawakened by Morgan Wylie
Somewhere Within by Amy Hale

COMING SOON ARE books from Michele G. Miller, Cameo Renae, Randi Cooley Wilson, E.J. Fechenda, and more.

IMMERSE yourself in the world of Havenwood Falls and stay up to date on news and announcements at www.HavenwoodFalls.com. Join our reader group, Havenwood Falls Book Club, on Facebook at https://www.facebook.com/groups/HavenwoodFallsBookClub/

ABOUT THE AUTHOR

Kristen has always had an intense fear of water—maybe it can be attributed to the dark world of sirens lurking under the surface of her subconscious. Or it's just because she cannot swim. When she isn't reading and writing, she's exploring creepy historical things with her daughter or attempting to cook (it's debatable which is scarier). You can find her on Facebook, Instagram, and Twitter. Oh, and if you're a dude going swimming in the wild, don't forget to bring a rubber inner-tube—it could buy you a couple of minutes.

ACKNOWLEDGMENTS

God, thank you for leading me here and allowing this to even happen.

Thank you to my parents, my Gramps, my Grams and Great-Grams (who fervently believed in my stories since I was too little for them to make sense), Aunt Jackie, Aunt Colleen, Nate, Shaina, Jen, Steven, Sean, and Damien for forever love.

Ryan, the last time that we were together before you died, I swore that I would follow through on this dream. A promise is a promise, little bro. Thank you for the years of mischief managed. I will miss you for the rest of my days.

Thank you to my own "Mr. Weaver" for seeing in me what I couldn't see when I was in high school.

Andrew Smith, your taste in indie music is impeccable. Nikki wouldn't be Nikki without your musical guidance, thank you! Jay Asher—you started out as one of my favorite authors, turned mentor, turned friend. You were there for me during some of the worst times of my life, encouraging me to keep writing, and to be kind to myself. Thank you for all you have done for me, and for so many others in this world.

Tina Sandoval and Tiffany Neal, "No, read *this* one." I would be lost without you both on the written page and off. Sam Sandoval—

thanks for being my forever-teen-reader. Gina Kupfer, Amy Viscuso, and Chrystal Mook, thank you for cheering me on!

Regina Wamba, thank you for making Serena and me feel like princesses with this gorgeous cover!

Liz Ferry, thank you for polishing up my words!

A special thank you goes out to all the Havenwood Falls authors. Thank you, E.J. Fechenda, Randi Cooley Wilson, Kristie Cook, Michele G. Miller, and Kallie Ross for sharing your characters with me!

Kristie Cook, when you offered for me to take part in this, it was too good to be true. Guess what? I finished. Thank you for believing I could!

Alexa, my baby girl, thank you for being the Rory to my Lorelai. P.S.: It's a belt bag.

Last but certainly not least, thank *you* for spending your precious minutes and hard-earned money on me and my imaginary friends. You are the reason that I do what I do!

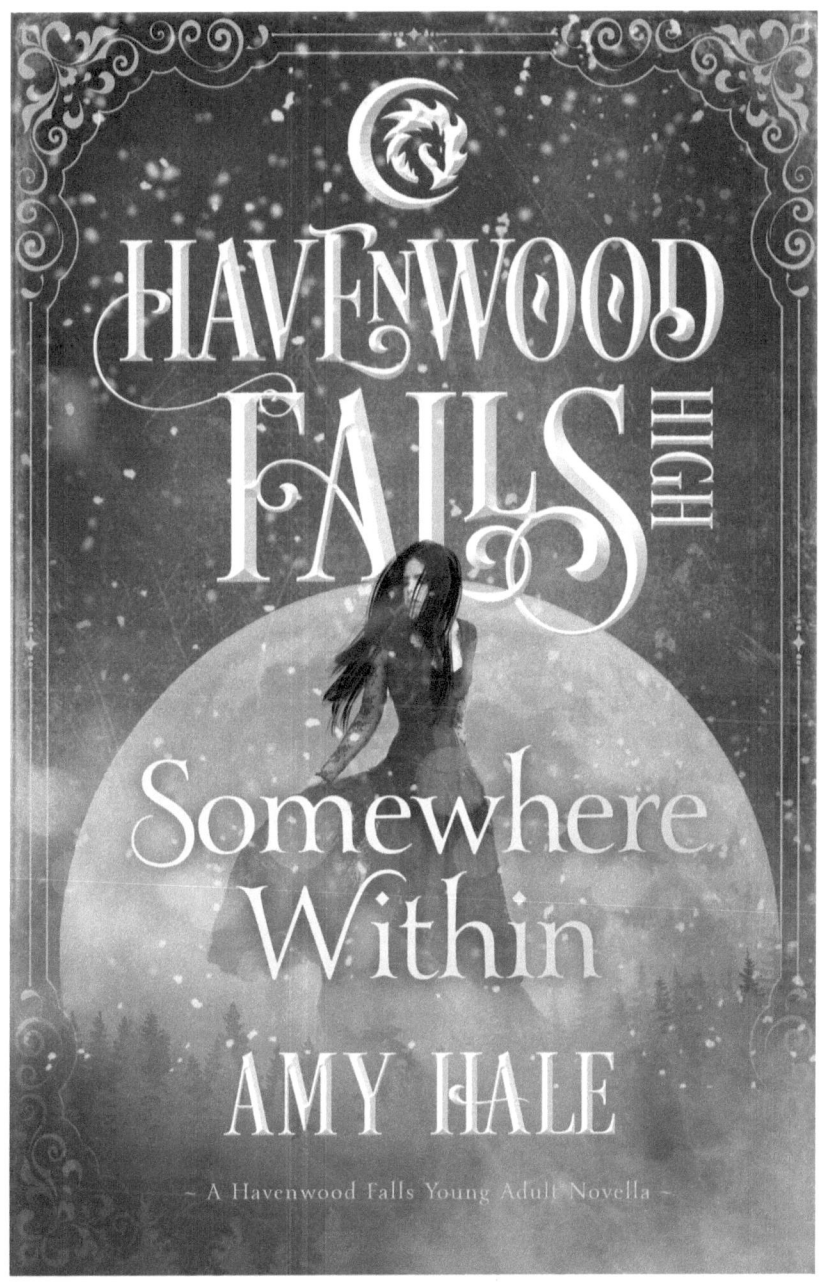

HAVENWOOD FALLS HIGH

Somewhere Within

AMY HALE

~ A Havenwood Falls Young Adult Novella ~

Somewhere Within (A Havenwood Falls High Novella) by Amy Hale

With her raven-black hair, porcelain-white skin, and shy demeanor, Zoey Mills has been the target of bullies since childhood, no matter how many times her family moved. She expects nothing to change when they relocate to Havenwood Falls, her parents' hometown. What she doesn't expect is to discover that she inherited her eccentricities— as the next generation of a long line of frost dragons.

As she learns to accept she's on the cusp of becoming a shifter, she finds out her new best friend isn't human, either. But the boy Zoey's fallen for is, earning the disapproval of her grandfather and patriarch and fueling the fire of a decades-long feud among her extended family. Elitism and prejudice take on whole new meanings.

While she wants to trust her instincts and follow her heart, Zoey discovers that hiding who she really is and playing by the rules would make life a lot simpler. But simple doesn't mean easy. She must find her strength somewhere within and embrace her destiny—or risk losing everyone she cares about. And all of this on the eve of her Sweet Sixteen.

SOMEWHERE WITHIN

AN EXCERPT

I glanced at the boxes still waiting to be unpacked as I attempted to relax in my new bedroom. The excitement that generally accompanied a new house was missing. I felt like we moved more than we stayed still. My dad had assured me this would be the last time, and while I thought he believed that to be true, I had my reservations.

My first memories of moving took place at age seven. I don't remember all the details, but I do recall a loud commotion, after which Mom had run out to the backyard to get me. She rushed me into the car, and we left. Just like that. No goodbyes to the neighbors. No "grab a few things for overnight." We just left. Two days later, my dad arrived at our hotel room, two states away, driving a moving truck containing all our belongings. At the time, I was afraid to ask what happened, but it had certainly crossed my mind with every successive move. I'd had an unpleasant sensation down in my gut each time I attempted to mention the subject, so I'd always chickened out.

So there I was, on move . . . what was it? Move eight? Yeah, I thought this was move number eight. One would think I'd be used to starting over, and over, and over. But the truth was that with every packed box, I felt like I'd left a part of me behind. Even if that part wasn't important, it was a segment of my scattered life that no longer felt valid. Those memories now lived in the past.

This latest move had been prompted by a family member. It turned out I had a grandfather here in Havenwood Falls, Colorado. My parents had never talked about him before, so I'd assumed my dad didn't know who his father was. It was the only logical explanation for never hearing about Grandpa Mills. You couldn't talk about someone you didn't know, right?

My parents had received a letter that my grandfather, Lawrence Mills, had become very ill, and was possibly dying. Mom and Dad seemed frustrated by the phone conversations they'd had with him afterward. Ultimately, I held the impression they'd decided it was time to mend fences. Granted, they'd never told me what busted the fences to begin with, but maybe someday I'd learn all the deep, dirty family secrets. All families had a skeleton or two in their closets, so I'd heard. I suspected my family to be no different.

I stood and opened the box closest to my bed. It contained some of my clothes and the most beautiful jewelry box I'd ever seen. It'd been a gift from my parents for my sixteenth birthday. I hadn't actually had that birthday yet, but it was only about a month away. Dad had said that he wanted to give it to me before the move. "Something special for your new room," he'd said. I thought he'd been attempting to bribe me so I wouldn't complain about changing houses and schools yet again. It kinda worked.

I ran my fingers over the smooth metal casing, and I could almost feel it vibrate beneath my fingers. I didn't know how to explain it, but it felt as if the box itself was alive. Every time I touched it, I felt a zing of positive energy pulse through me. No doubt these sensations all took place in my mind, but I allowed myself to indulge the fantasy just the same. As long as I didn't say it out loud, I should be safe. Admitting it to others would have been like saying I'd grown a third leg, but no one could see it.

I placed the gold box on my nightstand and studied the intricate design on the lid, which looked much like a maze, with lines darting out from the center in odd geometric patterns. From the moment I laid eyes on it, I'd tried to figure out if there were some kind of labyrinth hidden in all the chaos, but if so, I had yet to solve it.

Regardless, it was another great addition to what my mother lovingly called my "jewelry hoard." I did have a slight obsession with jewelry, but really, what teenage girl didn't? I wouldn't call it a hoard.

"Zoey, here's another box with your name on it." Dad pushed through my bedroom door and set the box on the bed beside me. "Sheesh, that's heavy. What do you have in there? Anvils?"

I rolled my eyes at him. "Yes, Father. I have an anvil addiction. You've found me out."

He smirked. "So much sass in such a little person."

I reached over and pulled the tape from the top of the box, then glanced inside. "Oh," I said.

Dad simply raised his eyebrows in curiosity.

"It's my jewelry boxes," I said quietly.

His soft laughter followed him to the door, and he sent me a wink. "Enjoy." He walked out of the room and gently closed the door behind him.

I looked into the box again. I had several jewelry boxes, most of them very full. *Okay, maybe I do have a jewelry-hoarding issue. Is there a therapy for that?*

AFTER LUNCH, Dad had some things to take care of at his new job running Simple Treasures Pawn Shop, so that left just Mom and me cleaning and unpacking in the kitchen.

Mom crossed her arms and leaned against the tan Formica counter. "What do you say we run into town for coffee? A latte sounds great, and I noticed a nice-looking shop as we drove through town."

I put away the last plate in the stack I'd unpacked and wiped my hands on my jeans. "Sure. Sounds good."

She smiled at me. "Perfect. As much as I love this new house, I'm eager to get out for a few minutes."

I didn't comment. I knew she wanted to hear me gush about the new place. After all, it was a nice house. A relatively new brick ranch house, it contained three bedrooms and loads of extra space. My bedroom easily overshadowed the dimensions of any other room I'd ever had. I even had my own bathroom. The pale yellow walls and white gauzy curtains gave my room a cheery feel. My white bedroom suite fit perfectly within the space. Much to my mother's delight, there were hardwood floors throughout. All I could think about was how cold those floors would be first thing in the morning. I made myself a mental note to ask for a rug in my bedroom.

The main part of the house had an open floor plan with the living room, kitchen, and dining room all in one large area. The fireplace had to be my favorite feature of the house, aside from my bedroom. The large grate could hold a decent-sized load of wood, and I could imagine the relaxing crackle as the flames warmed my fingers and toes while the smell of the fire saturated my clothes.

I had every reason to love our new home, yet all I could muster for my mother was a less-than-excited smile. As for the town—it was lovely. The gorgeous mountains surrounding the town boxed us in and lent a cozy, protected feel. As it was November, the air felt frigid and crisp, but also clean. Air this fresh was foreign to me, since all our other homes were in larger cities filled with smog and the various odors that accompanied living in a crowded area with several thousand people. One apartment had been so poorly located that a few times I wondered if I'd ever get the stench of garbage out of my nostrils. There was nothing like living a few blocks from a landfill when the wind blew just right. Thankfully, that stay was short-lived.

Havenwood Falls was perfectly sized for exploring. I hadn't had a chance to look everything over yet, but Mom assured me I could easily walk from one end of town to the other. Since I'd always felt pulled to the outdoors, I should have been thrilled, but moving and leaving what little stability we'd had dampened my spirits. The unknown was always scary. I'd never been good with change.

Mom pushed away from the counter. "C'mon, kiddo. Let's get some caffeine."

She wasn't kidding about the size of Havenwood Falls. We'd only been on the road a few minutes when we pulled into a spot in front of a collection of cute little storefronts on the town square. We stepped onto the sidewalk, and I glanced at the surrounding businesses. It seemed to be the typical small-town America kind of place, except for a few eclectic shops, which oddly didn't seem out of place. I spotted Madame Tahini's, whose sign advertised potions, palm readings, and other services. I couldn't say I'd ever been in a store like that. It intrigued me. It was at the end of the block, next to Simple Treasures Pawn Shop, which was owned by my grandfather and now managed by my dad.

Directly in front of our parking space was Coffee Haven. The bell over the door greeted us with the light tinkle of chimes as we entered the shop. The scent of coffee and baked goods hit me immediately. I was suddenly thankful for the distraction and the promise of chocolate. I wasn't as into the whole froufrou drink thing as my mom was. If it had a weird name and complicated list of ingredients, she'd try it. I honestly preferred hot cocoa over coffee. Thankfully, most coffee places offered both. With it being the first week in November, the weather was perfect for a warm drink.

I glanced around the cozy space, and my eyes were instantly drawn to a section near the back of the shop. Shiny silver, copper, and gold hung from various displays, and the overhead lights caused a sparkle from the beads and gems as I moved to the right or left. My quest for hot chocolate was all but forgotten.

"I see that look in your eye," Mom teased.

"What?" I shrugged. "I'm just looking around."

"Well, why don't you go look closer, and I'll order your drink. You want your usual? With peppermint?" She asked.

"Yeah, that'd be great. Thanks." I wasted no time in getting to the jewelry display. Several gorgeous pieces were front and center, and I couldn't help but reach out and touch them. I had an affinity for all jewelry, but these were expertly handcrafted by someone named Serena Alverson, and I found myself wishing I had such a creative gift. Of course, if I did, I'd likely end up with more jewelry than all the stores in town combined, so it was probably fortunate I didn't possess that talent.

I glanced down at the bracelet hanging from my wrist. It was my favorite, and my parents had gifted it to me on my tenth birthday. The green and yellow crystal beads were strung together on a delicate gold chain. Inside the gift box there had been a note indicating that the crystals were fluorite and yellow jasper, providing the dual function of an energy shield and a protective amulet. I wasn't sure I bought into all that, but I loved wearing it just the same.

"Zoey, here's your drink." My mom's voice pulled me from the allure of shiny objects, and she motioned for me to join her at a small table near the large picture window in front. My mother and I were opposites. Her short brown hair barely reached her shoulders, and her eye color matched it perfectly. Naturally petite, she possessed an inner grace and beauty. She preferred more casual clothing, but no matter what she wore, she made it look classy. She oozed charm and confidence. I did not. I was more comfortable reading in my room than I was socializing. Outside of us both having pale complexions and being short, I appeared to be nothing like her—a disappointing realization.

My dad was a tall man, easily over six feet in height with only a slightly darker skin tone and a muscular build. His hair had a thick texture with waves, and while dark, it was nowhere near the raven black of my own hair. His eyes were blue, where mine were gray with hints of blue. His self-assurance inspired me, and I had idolized him for as long as I could remember. He was my hero. I seemed so very different from them both. I often wondered if, upon my eighteenth birthday, they'd tell me I was adopted. It wouldn't have surprised me.

I took a seat opposite my mother and cupped the warm mug in my hands as I sipped it cautiously. Perfect. I looked up at the counter and noticed the young woman behind it smiling at me. Her name tag said Willow. *Such a pretty name!* I gave her a thumbs up to indicate my pleasure, and she winked at me, then turned to wipe down one of the espresso machines.

"So, what did you think of the jewelry? Anything you can't live without?" my mom asked as I took another careful sip of my drink.

"There are a few that are amazing, but I should probably at least get my room unpacked before I start adding more to my collection." I thought back to the various jewelry boxes in my room still waiting for my attention.

She laughed and reached across to pat my arm. Bad timing on her part, or on mine. As she moved, so did I—I scooted my mug to the side, directly in her path. Her fingers hit the cup and tipped it over, spilling the scalding hot contents all over my right hand.

I yelped in pain, and my mom jumped up to help me. Willow appeared at our side quickly, and I vaguely remembered hearing her ask how she could help. My instinct was to blow on the back of my hand, and to my amazement, impossibly cool air passed over my lips and cooled my skin. I watched in shock, and honestly some horror, as ice crystals formed over the burned area.

My mom wrapped her arms around me, shielding my hand and face from the view of those around us. A towel was thrust between our heads by a tight-smiled Willow.

"I've got this. Go take care of her before anyone notices." Willow's voice barely registered above a whisper.

She and my mom exchanged a look that I couldn't understand, then Mom nodded and ushered me out the door.

"It's okay, baby. Let's get you to the hospital to have that looked at." Mom spoke louder than necessary, and I began to think I was losing my mind—or dreaming.

The pain had disappeared, and I had a morbid eagerness to peek under the dish towel to see how bad my injury really was. I glanced back into the shop and saw Willow quickly cleaning up the mess we'd left behind.

It seemed like only seconds before I found myself sitting in the passenger seat as Mom backed out of her parking space.

I peeled the towel back from my hand, expecting to either see the worst, or see that I'd imagined the severe burn, but found nothing but a small mark. What I didn't expect to see . . . I didn't even know what it was. It was white, shimmery, and hard—almost like a shell.

Panic welled up in my chest. I struggled to breathe.

"Mom?" I could hear the fear in my own voice, so I knew she heard it too.

"It's okay, sweetheart. It's gonna be fine." She pulled out her cell phone and hit a button. "Call Tristan," she said loudly.

The phone answered back, "Calling Tristan Mills."

Mom put the phone to her ear and waited only a few seconds, then said, "Tristan, it's happening. Meet us at home as soon as you can."

I heard the muffled voice of my dad say, "On my way," and then the line went dead.

"Mom?" I asked again. "What is this? What's happening?"

She glanced at me and sighed a deep, worried-sounding breath. "It's a long story. Dad and I will explain it all when we get home."

We drove in silence until we reached our new house—not the hospital, by the way. My gut told me something big loomed before me. Something I was totally unprepared for.

PURCHASE *Somewhere Within* at your favorite book retailer.